# Bury Me A G 2

Tranay Adams

**Lock Down Publications
Presents
Bury Me A G 2
A Novel by *Tranay Adams***

# Lock Down Publications

P.O. Box 1482

Pine Lake, Ga 30072-1482

First Edition May 2015
Printed in the United States of America

**Lock Down Publications**
**Email:** tranayadams@gmail.com
**Facebook:** Tranay Adams
**Like our page on Facebook: Lock Down Publications**
@www.facebook.com/lockdownpublications.ldp
**Cover design and layout by:** Dynasty's Cover Me
**Book interior design by**: Shawn Walker
**Edited by:** Tumika Cain

## *Dedication*

My fifth novel is DEDICATED to my mother, Stella Ray. I will never settle down until I find a woman as incredible as you are.

I love you to life,

*Your Oldest.*

Tranay Adams

# Chapter One

"Say, you two brothas wouldn't happen to be Tiaz and Threat, now would ya?" the old man asked as he took pulls from the cigarette wedged between his fingers. The older gent was about sixty something rocking a porkpie hat and shades. He'd been posted up outside of the club that night singing songs and playing his guitar trying to make a living.

"Who wants to know?" Threat and Tiaz turned around with scowls plastered on their faces.

"That's confirmation enough." The old man said to no one in particular. He dropped the cigarette on the ground and mashed it out under the heel of his dress shoe. He sat up in his chair, gripping the guitar and clearing his throat. He swallowed then began to sing a song about the Grim Reaper coming to claim the souls of two men who were ignorant of his presence. Tiaz, Threat, Bianca and Chevy, their dates that night, watched the old man as he performed the ballad. The old man finished the last few bars of the song:

*He wears a hood over his head*
*a scythe with a blade 'bout as long as your leg*
*it's too late to scream 'cause you're already dead*
*what's understood doesn't have to be said*
*here he comes*
*here he cuuuuuhhmes*
*here he comes*
*here he cuuuuuhhmes*
*death awaits...*

The old man brushed his thumb and index finger across the strings of his guitar one last time, finishing the song. He then removed his hat and wiped the sweat from his forehead with the back of his hand.

The song unnerved everyone, the hairs on the back of their necks and arms stood up. Chills whisked back and forth through the air as if winter was coming, but if the thugs and their ladies thought that, then they were sadly mistaken. It wasn't winter that was coming, it was *Death*. Their hearts quickened and their bodies shivered like icicles were sliding down their backs. They were a bit shaken up.

"Who told you our names?" Threat's neck snapped in all directions, looking for a possible suspect. He wanted to know who it was that was after them right then. The sooner he knew, the faster they could put an end to the nigga.

"A smooth talking dude in a snazzy, purple suit described how you two brothas looked and gave me your names." The old man went on to tell them, with a triumphant expression written across his face, "He paid me a $100 dollars, uh huh." He took the time to pull a cigarette from the wrinkled pack in his breast pocket, putting it between his lips. "Told me to sing that song to you. It's an original, do you like it?"

Threat and Tiaz exchanged glances, realizing who the old man was talking about.

"What was his name? Did he tell you who he was?" Tiaz rattled off questions anxiously, ready to fuck the old man up if he didn't give him some answers. He clenched his fists tightly.

The old man lit up the cigarette, took a couple of puffs then blew out a roar of smoke. Shaking his head no, he replied, "Afraid not, gentlemen. The fella dropped a yard on me, described you two to the T and told me to sing that song to you when you came outta this here establishment." He motioned towards the club with the hand he held the cigarette in.

"Majestic," Bianca said, remembering the name. Threat and Tiaz turned around to her. "While we were dancing, he told me his name was Majestic."

The sound of a horn being honked startled everyone and caused them to turn towards the street. A limousine was there. Its windows were tinted too dark for anyone on the outs to peer inside. The back passenger side window slowly rolled down and exposed the face of the man hidden inside. It was Majestic, and he was smiling sinisterly. Instantly, his face morphed into a frown and he squared his jaws, moving to point something out of the window. Tiaz and Threat's eyes bugged and their mouths dropped open. They were frozen with terror and all they could do was wait for the shot that would end one of their lives. Tiaz and Threat had been faced with death more times than the number of years they'd been alive. It was safe to say that they didn't fear anything on God's green earth, not even him for that matter. But the terror that they felt at the time was unsuspecting. Shit, it even came as a shock to them.

Majestic's hand came up and out of the window, tossing out a bouquet of roses. The flowers bounced off of the sidewalk and skidded a little. Tiaz and Threat, who were standing in front of their women, to use themselves as human shields, looked down at the roses. They were reddish black and brittle. They were dead. This was a message. Their heads snapped up just in time to see the limousine driving off. Their faces twisted with anger and they clenched their fists. They were used to being the ones striking fear in niggaz' hearts, and now that they were on the receiving end they didn't like it, not one bit. They'd just experienced something that they'd never felt before, and that was vulnerability. No one had ever pulled their hoe cards, but it happened tonight.

Tiaz and Threat's eyes followed the backlights of the limousine as it drove away. They wished they hadn't left their head bussas in the car so they could have dumped on it.

"Punk ass mothafucka." Threat fumed and spat on the curb.

"Come on, let's go." A scowling Tiaz nudged him.

"Babe, what's going on?" Chevy questioned with worry written across her face.

"Now isn't the time for talking, we gotta get the fuck outta here." He spat sharply, grabbing his lady's hand and fleeing toward the valet parking lot, not wanting to wait around for valet to bring them the vehicle, in the event that Majestic came back. Threat was right behind them pulling Bianca on, his head on a swivel in case Majestic's ass came back around looking to claim their lives.

Tiaz and Threat were faced with a new opponent and they'd have to eliminate him before they both ended up in coffins.

***

"Tiaz, have you and Threat gotten yourselves into something in the streets that you haven't told me about?" Chevy asked as she began to remove her earrings.

"Nah, ain't nothing like that. Niggaz see my man, Threat, getting money and they hating. They see me standing next to him, so they throw shade my way, too," he replied, taking his blazer off. She had been quiet on their way back home from the club, but he had a feeling that she was going to start in on him once they'd gotten back home. That's why he concocted a decent story for when she came questioning him.

"Babe, something is going on and I need to know what it is." She unbuckled her sandals. She wasn't buying the bullshit story he was trying to sell her. "If me and Te'Qui are in some sort of danger, I need to make arrangements for us to stay somewhere else until I find another place to live. Is this some old street beef that's come back to haunt chu?" She began to remove her dress, one shoulder at a time. The house was strangely quiet, being that it was only the two of them and Te'Qui was at Baby Wicked's house.

Tiaz hung his blazer up inside of the closet and pulled off his Obey T-shirt. He blew hard as he kicked off his Chuck Taylor's, it had been a long night and he didn't really feel like talking, but he figured she deserved an explanation.

"We took Majestic for a few bricks before I went inside, that's why he's after us." He lied. He was afraid of telling her the truth for fear that she may stop fucking with him. The two of them had met through a website called Penpals.com and hit it off almost instantly. He was told that if he wanted to be with her then he had to promise to turn his back on the streets when he came home. He agreed thinking that he could keep his dealings hidden from her, but it was starting to look like his little secret could possibly get exposed.

Tiaz and Threat didn't make a move on Majestic until he was out of prison and even then they only came up on a few bands. There weren't any drugs of any type around when they'd broke bad. There was a hundred thousand in a duffle bag which they almost seized, until the cats that were guarding the stash house came out with them choppas busting on their asses. Still, he and Threat managed to escape with their lives and twenty racks. Although they still had a problem, one of the biggest coke dealers in Southern California was on them like stink on shit now. And he wouldn't stop until they both were lying with tombstones at their heads.

"Tee, Majestic ain't no joke, I've heard stories about him," she said, slipping into a tight fitting T-shirt and boy shorts.

"Well, your man ain't no joke either, especially when one of these are in my hand." His voice dripped with arrogance as he held up the banger that he'd just pulled from his waistline. He then stashed it under the mattress. He took off his jeans and pulled down his boxer briefs, exposing his nakedness. "Look. Don't worry, you won't have to move. Me and my nigga, Cam, are going to take care of Majestic." He kissed her on the forehead.

"That's what I'm afraid of," she said with saddened eyes.

"I live by an unwritten code of ethics, Love, so running to The Boys is not an option for me. Don't expect me to compromise. Now, I'ma catch this old nigga slipping and show'em how a real goon gets down. All I need for you to do is hold it down how you've been doing, alright?" She reluctantly nodded. He held her chin up to him and kissed her on the lips then grabbed the items he'd need for his shower and ducked off into the bathroom.

*Baby, I hope you keep to your word, 'cause God knows if I were to lose you my entire world would crumble. I've finally found a man that loves and appreciates me, and to have that taken away from me I'd...shut up, bitch! Stop thinking like that! Everything is going to be alright. Tiaz will take care of it. Like he said back in prison 'trust and believe in him.' That's exactly what I'ma do, too.*

Chevy sat on the bed looking over her French manicured fingernails. Hearing a cell phone vibrating, she looked to the closet. Her curiosity brought her to the closet where she listened closely for the vibrating phone, locating it inside of

Tiaz's blazer. She fished around inside of the blazer's pockets until she felt his cell phone. When she looked at the screen, she saw one missed call from Threat. While this was happening she could hear her boo singing in the bathroom. Curiosity got the best of her and she scrolled until she found the text messages. She looked through a series of text messages from Kantrell. Each one that she read made her feel like someone was kicking her in the heart, harder and harder. Her stomach twisted into knots, her chest tightened and she felt a stinging in her eyes. The flood gates opened and tears cascaded down her face.

"Why God? Why is this happening to me, yet again?" Her voice cracked under her emotions as she glanced up at the ceiling, questioning her Lord and Savior, feeling like she'd been through enough with her fiancé and finally deserved her piece of happiness.

Tiaz lied to her, shitted on her, having no regards to how she felt.

*"I'ma give you a love that's only been heard about in fairy tales. Trust and believe in me...I'ma give you the love you need, the love you want, the love you deserve. All I ask in return is for one thing."*

*"What?"*

*"That thing beating behind your left breastplate...that's right, your heart. That's all I want. That's all I need from you. You give me that and I promise with my right hand before God, I'll make you the happiest woman on the face of this earth."*

*"You mean it?"*

*"You're damn right I do."*

"You're just like the rest of them." She sobbed. "No fucking different. Asshole," she said in a hushed tone.

Wiping away her tears with the back of her hand, she scrolled over to the picture messages, but they just kept on coming. Chevy looked at several provocative pictures of her best friend. She went through about eight of them before rage began to build inside of her. Her face twisted into anger and her chest heaved as she breathed hard. With her blood-shot eyes and tear soaked face, she looked like a woman that had gone mad. Hearing the squeak of the shower water's dial as it was being turned off, she grabbed one of his thick leather belts from off the rack on the back of the bedroom door. She kicked open the bathroom door. *Boom.* She barged inside to find him wrapping a towel around his waist. She shoved his cell phone into his face, with Kantrell's provocative picture on display. He felt his stomach drop, his mouth opened to say something, but being caught red handed left his vocal cords paralyzed.

"What's wrong? Cat got your tongue?" she asked.

He looked from Kantrell's picture on the cell phone to her tear streaked face.

A light bulb came on inside of his head and what he believed was a reasonable explanation formed in his mind. "Baby, let me explain…" he held up his hands.

"Explain my ass!" she roared, whacking him across the face with the belt. The leather felt like Icy-Hot ointment on his skin, it burned. Tiaz bellowed in pain, he went to grab the side of his face, but the thought was derailed when she struck him with the belt again. He hollered out and went to grab her, but she stepped aside and kept with her assault on his hide. The thug spilled out into the hallway, he held up his hands and legs trying to block the rain of the belt. His buff ass was still wet, so the stings of it felt like a whip engulfed in flames. Red bruises and welts began to form on his arms, legs and body. His face grimaced as she assaulted him with vigorous anger, talking shit as she beat him like he was an unruly slave on her plantation. He lost his towel in the tussle and ended up butt naked. He managed to grab a hold of the belt and tripped her up. She fell on her back and he straddled her, holding her hands down by both of her wrists.

"Calm the fuck down, man! I'm tryna tell yo' crazy ass what happened!" Tiaz barked, raining spittle in her face.

"You don't have to tell me shit! You aren't any different from Faison!" Chevy hollered back in his face. "Let me go!"

"No! I'm not letting you go until you calm down and listen to me!" He demanded of her, knowing he'd fucked up big time and there was a good chance that he'd lose her.

At that precise moment, his face turned red and veins formed in his forehead and neck. He felt a pain that couldn't be explained when she kneed him in his balls. She shoved him off of her person and he fell aside, holding his family jewels. He bawled on the floor as she got to her feet and kicked him in the stomach, knocking the wind out of him.

Chevy's chest heaved up and down as she stared down at Tiaz angry, yet calm at the same time. Her eyes turned red and glassy, her nostrils expanding and shrinking. She looked like she was possessed by the Exorcist Demon.

"I want you and yo' shit outta my house before I get back. If you're still here when I return, I'm gonna shoot you in yo' face, do you hear me? I'm not gonna listen to you and yo' bullshit excuse! I'm gonna waltz right up on you and pull the mothafucking trigger." She stormed off to the bedroom. When she returned, she was wearing jeans and sneakers and shoving her Taurus .9mm into her purse. She stood over him as he bawled, holding his precious family stones. He wanted to tax that ass, but the pain left him paralyzed. Then again, he felt like he deserved it, he'd done to her what he promised not to, fuck with her heart.

"I thought you were different, Tiaz. I thought we could really have something special together. I will never get chu men. You claim you want a ride or die chick, but just as soon as you get one you treat her like shit." She shook her head with disappointment and said, "Have a nice life, asshole!"

Ooof! She kicked him in the ribs before walking out of the door.

***

*Thung! Thung! Thung! Thung!*
Chevy's trunk rattled as the infectious throwback tune pumped from her Bose 12x12 subwoofer speakers.

*What is this I see (No)*
*You don't come home to me (Oh, no)*
*When you don't come home to me (Man)*
*Can't deal, can't bear*
*You keep tellin' lies*
*But to your surprise*
*Look I found her red coat*
*And your(bitch) caught out there*
*I hate you so much right now*
*I hate you so much right now*
*I hate you so much*
*Right now. Ahh...*

She listened to Kelis's *I hate you* on her drive to Kantrell's house. Although she wasn't crying anymore, her eyes were still bloodshot. Now she was cool, calm and collected. She had to focus, to be on point, if she was going to get some get-back. She drove one house down from her best friend's house, executed the engine, pulled her hair back into a ponytail, and took her gun out of her purse. As she looked from Kantrell's crib to the gun in her hand, she debated whether or not she should knock on the door and blast on her ass.

Chevy took a deep breath and exhaled, putting the gun back inside of her purse. There was no way she was about to kill this hoe over some dick, that would make her a weak bitch. Nah, she had to be smarter than that. She had a son she had to take care of and it wouldn't be fair to him if she were to do something that would jeopardize her freedom. Chevy picked up her cell phone and scrolled through her contacts until she found the trifling bitch's number. After clearing her throat, she then pressed the *call* button and readied herself to put on an Oscar worthy performance.

"Kantrell, me and Tiaz got into it." She faked sobbing. "Do you think I could spend the night at your house? Good, I'm parked outside. I'm finna come in now." After she disconnected the call, a devilish smile broadened her face. Once she hopped out of the car, she slammed the door closed and made sure her sneakers were laced tight. She walked up the steps and knocked on the door of her best friend's home. A moment later, she heard the door being unlocked.

\*\*\*

He parked the G-ride around the corner from her house and killed the engine. He placed a neoprene mask on the lower half of his face and pulled the drawstrings of his hood, closing it around his head. His gloved hand dipped beneath the driver seat and came back up clutching a chrome .45 with a black silencer. Once he made sure it was locked and loaded, he hopped out of the stolen car and crept up the driveway of the house next door. He hopped the back gate of the house and landed into the backyard of Kantrell's crib. Moving as stealthy as a thief, he tiptoed up the steps of the back porch. Tucking his weapon into the small of his back, he took the pins he'd need to pick the lock. Having gotten the door open, he snuck into the house, smiling sinisterly, as he withdrew the gun from around his back. When he emerged into the kitchen's doorway he could see the back of Kantrell's head as she watched TV. The living room was dark and the illumination of the television outlined her head.

*Yeah, bitch, I told you that you weren't getting away with that shit,* he thought as he lifted his weapon to deliver the kill shot. Dude was still pissed off about her having shot at him, making him walk the streets asshole naked. There wasn't any way in hell he was letting her get off the hook with that shit. Fuck all of that, he had a reputation to uphold. The intruder was about to pull the trigger when Kantrell's cell phone rang. He lowered his gun and hid beside the doorway, occasionally peeking around the corner into the living room. He watched as she talked on the cell for a time before unlocking and opening the door.

"Chevy, are you..." Kantrell was cut short by a crushing punch to the center of her face. The assault caused a sharp pain to shoot through her face and for her to see a flash of white. She staggered backwards, holding her broken and spurting nose. Chevy ran into the house and kicked her dead in the chest. The impact sent blood flying from out of her nose and her sailing back into the glass table in the living room.

*Crash!* The table exploded and sent shattered glass everywhere, tendrils of flowers lay strewn from a ceramic vase.

Kantrell scrambled to her feet, cutting up her hands and arms, shards of glass crunching at her feet. "Bitch, you were supposed to have been my best friend, my mothafucking sister!" Chevy screamed, spittle flying from her lips. She kicked her in the ribs, making her holler out and fall against the couch. As she went to stomp her head, Kantrell kicked her leg out from under her, she hit the floor on her back. When she looked up, Kantrell was running from out of the kitchen with a chair. She was in the motion of bringing it down on her face. Chevy rolled out of the way, missing the chair by an inch, springing to her feet.

"Trifling ass hoe! You wanna hit people with shit? Square up!" she bellowed, loose strands of hair in her face looking like she'd just woken up. *This bitch ain't just tryna fight, this trick tryna kill me,* she thought, seeing the rage in her ex-homegirl's eyes. She looked like a wild ass hyena.

"Ahhh, fuck you!" Kantrell swung her fist in a backward motion trying to crack her in the jaw. She ducked her advance and gave her two to the body and one to the head. Kantrell staggered back on the broken glass that polluted the floor, but quickly regained her equilibrium. She squared up with her opponent, hands dripping blood from her injuries. The girls went at it like grown men. There wasn't any scratching, slapping or hair pulling. They got down like a couple of niggaz in the street.

Kantrell assaulted Chevy with a three punch combination to the face. The blonde bombshell shook it off and struck back with a combination of her own. Homegirl set Kantrell up with two jabs to the face and then a sharp left. After two body shots came a right hook that made her scummy ass buckle. Chevy went to lunge at her and she kicked her in the chest with a force that sent her slamming into the wall and causing a portrait to fall.

"Uh huh, come on, bitch!" Kantrell's pupils were ablaze as she motioned her over with bloody hands.

"Grrrrrr!" Chevy unleashed a guttural growl as she raged forth.

As the women were about to collide, he swung out into the kitchen doorway gripping his silenced .45 with both hands. He smiled fiendishly, licking his lips as he applied pressure to the trigger of his weapon.

*Choot!*

A hole the size of a nickel opened between his eyes as his head snapped back. His eyes bulged and his mouth formed an O. He collapsed to the floor and his gun spun around in circles until it bumped up against the refrigerator. Chevy and Kantrell froze with surprise written across their faces. Their heads whipped all around until their eyes landed on Tiaz. He was aiming his silenced smoking Beretta over their heads, a black garbage bag lay at his feet. Chevy looked to the kitchen floor and locked eyes with a familiar face. Zooming in on it, she couldn't believe that it was him. It couldn't be. Her eyes were playing tricks on her. They had to be. Her eyes widened and her jaw dropped in devastation. Her lips moved, but her mouth couldn't form the words on her mind. Finally, she spoke the dead man's name.

"Azule!" she croaked, bereaved. This was her dude after her failed engagement to Faison, the hustler that wanted to be anything and everything like him. She'd always thought that he'd packed up his shit and moved out of Cali, but here his ass was lying dead as shit in her bestie's kitchen. Confusion masked her face. She looked from her former boo's lifeless form to her best friend. Her forehead creased with lines and her eyes asked what was on her brain. Kantrell's scandalous ass confirmed it.

"Yeah, I was fucking 'em, too!" She twisted her lips and moved her neck like a chicken head, folding her arms across her chest. Azule wasn't all she thought he would be. She believed he was a real prize since her girl had him, but boy was she wrong. Although the Faison knockoff did take good care of her and give her that good good, the nigga had a problem with putting his mothafucking hands on her. Now, don't get it tangled and twisted, she wasn't just letting him go upside her head, nah, she was chunking them with his big ass, too. But what chance could she stand against him? He was a man and she was a woman. Kantrell didn't know who she was mad at the most: herself for snatching Azule's unruly ass or Chevy for making it so easy for her to take her man.

"Bitch!" Chevy clenched her teeth and threw one. *Crack!* A ripple went through Kantrell's cheeks and her eyelids turned into slits. She flipped over the couch, but came right back up wiping the blood from her lips. When she saw red smeared across her fist, her face contorted with hostility. Her nostrils inflated and deflated as she roared, jumping over the couch. Tiaz caught her in midair as she leaped, wrapping his arm around her as she struggled to get loose, kicking, swinging and screaming.

"Calm down. Calm the fuck down!" he grumbled in her ear, tight jawed. "We've gotta dead body in here we gotta get rid of." Although Kantrell could have easily claimed self defense since Azule broke into the house, Tiaz was the one that handed him his Death Certificate. He was a felon with an unregistered handgun he'd just bodied a nigga with. They'd be looking to throw his black ass under the jail.

Hearing this settled Kantrell down. She and Chevy locked eyes, intensity passing through them. The tension was so thick that it could be cut through with a Gemstar. "Baby, close the door."

"I'm not cha fucking baby. Not anymore!" she snapped.

"Now ain't the time, sweetheart, we've gotta get rid of this dead nigga in case The Ones pull up."

Chevy closed her eyes and took a deep breath, nodding her understanding.

"What do you want us to do?"

Tiaz looked around the living room. Spotting the oriental floor rug, he tucked his banger in the small of his back. He waved the girls over and said, "Y'all come on and help me move this furniture. We gon' wrap his ass up in this." The girls went to help him move the furniture. "Wait!" he blurted, stopping them in their tracks. "Kantrell, before we get started we need to take care of those hands and stop your nose from bleeding."

"I'm straight." She waved him off.

"No, you're not!" he stated sternly. "Get the first aid kit so I can take care of your wounds. Now!"

Kantrell was about to buck, but realizing how serious the matter was at hand with disposing the dead body, she decided to do like he said. Smacking her lips, she left and returned with the medical box. Tiaz cleaned her wounds and wrapped up her hands, he then plugged her nose with gauze.

Afterwards, she and Chevy assisted Tiaz in moving the furniture off of the rug, they placed Azule's body on it and used a towel to lay his gun down on his chest. They wrapped the corpse up in it and drug it to the back porch.

"Where's yo' ride parked at?" Tiaz asked Kantrell, panting out of breath.

"It's in the driveway," she answered, huffing and puffing.

"Driveway?" He frowned, remembering how she'd claimed she'd been jacked for her whip some time ago. It was on that same day that she gave him some scalp. "I thought you said it got..."

She cracked a satanic smile and shook her head. "Nahhh."

"Skeeza," he said under his breath.

"I heard that, and nigga, you ain't no betta than me, which cha bed hopping ass."

"Whatever. We don't have time for this shit," he said annoyed. "Bring yo' car around back, we're gon' drop 'em in the trunk and drive out into the woods to bury his ass."

Kantrell mad dogged Chevy as she approached her, throwing her shoulder into hers in passing. Chevy was about to put hands on her until Tiaz spoke up.

"Not now, y'all, come on we gotta get this shit done and out the way."

Kantrell brought her ride around to the back. They laid black garbage bags down inside of the trunk and dumped the load inside. They scrubbed and mopped the floors. They got a bag of lye and three shovels out of the tool shed, loaded it and drove out into the woods. Finding a place to bury Azule's dead ass, Tiaz sat the lantern down.

"Chev,' you keep an eye out while we digging," he ordered. Chevy nodded and headed off to watch for any witnesses.

Kantrell looked from Chevy to Tiaz. "Oh, so she gets to play guard dog, while I tend to the body? I see you still got cho nose up this bitch pussy, out here playing favoritism and shit."

"Knock it off." He picked up two shovels, passing her one. She rolled her eyes and blew hard, stabbing her shovel into the ground.

"You know what chu gotta do, right?" she asked in a hushed tone.

"Fuck you mean?" his brows furrowed. He'd already betrayed Chevy's trust and reopened old wounds, there was no way he was going to further persecute her by murking her out.

"She's gotta go, for both our sakes."

"Are you fucking serious?" His face twisted like *I can't believe you.*

"Yes, I'm fucking serious! How do we know she isn't gon' talk? Especially now that she's found out that I was fucking not one, but both of her niggaz."

He narrowed his eyes at her and angled his head. He couldn't believe she'd suggested that they nod her bestie. "Do you hear yo' self? You talking about putting the love on yo' best friend."

"Pleeeease, I ain't even tryna hear that. You see my face…" she pointed to her bruises. "Would a best friend do this to me? I think not. That bitch gotta go, Tiaz. She's the only thing standing between us and three hots and a cot, ya feel me?"

Kantrell had a seriously warped way of thinking. She felt like she could do any and everything to anybody without having to worry about the consequences. *The self righteous bitch!*

"No, I don't feel you," he grumbled. "I'm not touching her and that's final." He looked to see if Chevy was watching, she wasn't.

"Oh, really?"

"Yes, really." He gripped the shovel's handle tighter, his jaws pulsating angrily.

They held one another's glare for a time before she looked away. She rolled her eyes and blew hard, continuing her digging.

*Ol' pussy whipped ass nigga, scared to put this hoe to sleep. Well, he's gotta 'notha thing coming if he thinks I'ma leave this loose end untied. I ain't bout to let this shit ride, that's on my mothafucking daddy, rest in peace.*

"That's what I thought." He went on digging.

Sometime later Kantrell stabbed the shovel into the ground and looked at her palms, they were starting to blister.

"She's gotta take over. My hands are blistering."

"Alright." He nodded, breathing heavily. "Chev,' you're up, ma."

Chevy and Tiaz went at it until they had a six foot plot at their feet. They stabbed their shovels into the ground. Tiaz went to grab the body out of the trunk while she stood up panting with her hands on her hips. He'd just popped the trunk of Kantrell's BMW when he saw a flicker of movement out the corner of his eye. When he whipped around, she was just creeping up on Chevy, gun at her side.

"Yeah, bitch!"

"Huh?" Chevy whipped around just as the .32 was raised to her eye level. She gasped and her eyelids snapped open. Before she could utter a response, Kantrell was smiling wickedly and pulling the trigger. *Bow!*

The small pistol fired into the air and she grimaced as she was tackled to the ground. Tiaz picked up her weapon and rose to his feet, looking down at her like she had shit sliding down her face.

"Fuck is the matter with chu, girl?" He tucked the little gun into his pocket. He looked to Chevy. "You alright?" She nodded yes, hand over her chest. She couldn't believe that bitch had just tried to take her life.

He scooped up the carpet containing the body and dropped that bitch into the six foot hole. "Grab a shovel, Chev.' The more the merrier. Let's get this sucka buried and get ghost." With that order, they got the job done and took their leave.

The ride back to the house was a long and quiet one. Tiaz focused on the road, while Chevy stared out of the back passenger side window, watching the streets pass her by. Occasionally, she'd glance up and see Kantrell mad dogging her through the rearview mirror mouthing threats.

"You dead, bitch, you dead." She mouthed.

"Trust, this here ain't what chu want." Chevy mouthed back.

"We gon' see about that."

Chevy focused her attention back out of the window. An hour later, Tiaz was pulling back up at Kantrell's house. Before he could murder the engine Chevy was hopping out in a hurry and he was right behind her.

"Let that bitch go, Tiaz!" Kantrell hollered out as she was stepping out of her car. She didn't give a fuck about drawing attention, seeing as how they just covered up a murder and had evidence in the trunk that could have them all with lengthy prison stays.

"Shut cho fucking mouth!" He shot a finger at her. "Chev,' let me holla at chu for a minute."

Chevy whipped around with her face twisted up, jaws rigid.

"What?" she snapped.

He stepped closer, his hot breath moistening her face. "I trust that this is going to stay between us." He looked at her like *right?*

*Well, ain't this about a... This mothafucka got the audacity to ask me to keep his secrets quiet when he and his lil' tramp are the reason behind all of this shit? This Negro must have slipped and busted his goddamn head. Fuck him!*

Her eyes lowered, her nose flared and her lips twisted. She coiled her head and pursed her lips, throat rolling up and down.

*Hawk!* He squeezed his eyelids shut as the saliva splattered against his face, rolling and dripping off of his nose. She then went on about her business, heading over to her car. She hopped in and resurrected the Caprice, holding up a middle finger as she drove off.

"See, what the fuck I'm talking about, man?" Kantrell looked from the Chevrolet to Tiaz. "We gon' have to slump that hoe, straight like that!"

Tiaz turned back around and marched back toward the house, wiping his face with the inside of his T-shirt. Kantrell was right on his heels, trying to convince him to kill her best friend.

\*\*\*

"This nigga not answering, I'll just holla at him tomorrow." Threat sat his cell phone on the dresser and pulled his gun from the small of his back. He laid it in place of his pillow and then laid his pillow on top of it then went about his business, peeling off his clothes as Bianca sat on the edge of the bed smoking weed through a lime green glass bong, wearing only her black bra and panties. She placed the lighter to the smoking agent and took a couple deep pulls, emitting fogs from her nostrils and mouth. She coughed a little with the weed having been as potent as it was. When she looked up, her man was sliding into bed. He reached for the lighter and bong and she relinquished it to his possession. She watched as he went on to smoke from it, handling his like a young Snoop Dogg.

"Threat, is Majestic someone that we need to be worried about?" Her brows bunched together and wrinkled her forehead. She couldn't help to ask, given what had gone down at the club that night.

Threat blew smoke from his nose and let a fog roll off of his tongue before responding.

"Nah, he's someone that *I* need to be worried about." He corrected her. "Don't wet it, boo. Me and my nigga, Tiaz, gone take care of that."

"I'm just saying, bae, if there's something you want me to do to help you, I will." She spoke honestly. The look in her eyes told him that she was down to do whatever he asked of her.

"Aww, baby, you really mean that?" He cracked a grin, amused by her offer.

"Yes." She smiled sweetly.

"Good. Then shut the fuck up and suck my dick." He threw the covers from off his person and there his dick was standing through the hole of his boxer briefs, thick with veins running throughout it. She looked from him to his dick and back again, sliding her wet tongue across her top lip, seductively. She loved when he talked that gangsta shit to her, all rough and rugged. It made her coochie clench. As soon as her slick mouth engulfed his meat, he laid back and continued to smoke on the bong. He closed his eyes, enjoying the effects of the high and the scenery of the paradise she'd sent him to.

Bury Me A G 2

## Chapter Two

Baby Wicked stood before the nightstand mirror practicing drawing his .38 special from his waistline that his brother had given him before he'd gotten locked up. He'd pull the pistol from his waistline and point it at the mirror. He did this several times, trying to shorten the draw time with every try. He wanted to be swift on the draw when Maniac and Time Bomb came back around. The Crips had caught him and Te'Qui off guard when they rolled up on them while they were posted up trying to get it. They warned them to stay out of their territory and threatened to murder them if they ever caught them on their soil again. Baby Wicked felt like they got marked out. The way the young Locs got at them had him feeling like a straight up bitch. He hated that shit and he wasn't gone let it happen again. Shit, he couldn't let it happen again, because next time they could possibly end up dead.

Baby Wicked had to be ready when that beef came his way. He was dealing with killers who were in a league of their own. They'd murdered more men than he could count on the fingers of both of his hands. They'd perfected the art of murder, while he wasn't even a novice. So he had to be on point when the drama jumped off again. His and Te'Qui's lives depended on it.

"How long are you going to keep that up?" Te'Qui asked as he broke down Kush buds upon a Source magazine. The juveniles were free to get as high as they wanted off of Baby Wicked's older brother's stash. Aunt Helen was in the living room entertaining company and she'd never enter her nephew's bedroom without knocking first. Not to mention, they were burning a fragranced oil called *Butt Naked* which had a wonderfully strong scent of its own.

"'Til I'm the fastest gun on the Eastside," Baby Wicked answered. "You need to practice too, since we're going to be trading places back and forth while we're out there."

"I will." Te'Qui sprinkled the Kush inside of the blunt and licked it closed.

"Moms know that you're spending the night?"

"Yeah, she went out to some club with Tiaz and his homie, Threat," he replied, taking a pull from the blunt.

"Here, nigga, you try it." Baby Wicked passed him the .38 and took the blunt from him. He watched Te'Qui practice his drawing while he smoked on the blunt.

They had to be ready for the Avalon's this time, their lives would be at stake.

### *Later that night*

Te'Qui lay on the floor, while Baby Wicked lay above him on his bed. The boys lay with their hands behind their heads and staring up at the ceiling, chopping it up.

"You not worried just a lil' bit about being out there like that?" Te'Qui inquired.

"A lil,' but we got that thang-thang and this time ya boy gon' be on point." He spoke with bravado, sure everything was going to be fine.

"I hear you, but what if something goes wrong?"

He adjusted himself in bed, propping his fist against his head. "Like what?"

"What if one of us gets killed?"

"Oh," Baby Wicked stated. He hadn't thought about that. "It can happen. Pray for the best, but expect the worse. You feel me?"

His words came from a real place. He knew that the life he and others like him were living was a dangerous one. Shit could go left real fast and one could easily find himself in a coffin being lowered into the ground. The lucky ones became victims being rolled on a gurney into the back of an ambulance. That was just how it was, wasn't need for complaining. Bangers were schooled to the game before they were initiated.

"True that." He lay back down in bed. "But we're gon' get them chains come hell or high water."

The sole reason for Baby Wicked and Te'Qui hustling were for these gold chains that they had their eyes on at the Slauson Supermall. Although trying to post up and go hand to hand on someone else's turf to run that money up was risky, the boys felt like it was worth it if they were going to be able to floss their jewelry. Never mind Maniac almost murdering their young asses that day. They wanted those chains and no one could tell them that catching a bullet wouldn't be worth it.

"Is it really worth it though, the price of our lives?" Te'Qui questioned. He caught visions of his mother sobbing over his coffin and having to be torn from it by loved ones, kicking and screaming.

*"Take me, Lord, take me! Please, not my baby!"*

Hearing his mother's sorrowful screams inside of his head, he squeezed his eyelids shut and shook his head. He was trying to shake the thoughts from out of his mental. He knew that she'd be all broken up if he was to get killed out in the streets, but he wanted what he wanted. And he was willing to do whatever he had to do to get it in his possession.

"You wanna be from the set, don't chu?"

"Yep."

"Well, is it worth yo' life?"

Te'Qui didn't respond. He took the time to think to himself and realized that he wasn't quite sure if being down with the Bloods was really worth his life or not. As his young mind processed this, all that could be heard were the crickets in the grass outside and the occasional passing car.

"Exactly." He continued. "Life's a risk, homeboy. Every time you step foot outta yo' house you're looking not to come back."

Baby Wicked spoke with the knowledge of someone twice his age. This came from his limited experiences and hanging around his brother and his homies. He was like a sponge absorbing anything and everything from the seasoned gangstas, and then regurgitating it to his best friend.

"Real life."

"Anything can happen in this game we're playing, so if my enemies steal me from this world. Don't cry for me, ride for me, homie, straight up." He extended his hand and he sat up. They gave each another a complex handshake. "Night, my nigga." Baby Wicked turned over, pulling the covers over him.

"Night." Te'Qui stared up at the ceiling thinking to himself, watching and listening to the squeaky, white fan as it spun around in a blur. He still wanted into the Bloods, that was without a shadow of a doubt. Whatever he had to do to get in, he was down for it. As long as Baby Wicked had his back, he was ready to tackle whatever situations were set before him.

*God, watch over me and my homeboy as we look for all of the right ways to do the wrong things.* He closed his eyes.

\*\*\*

The hospital room was dimly lit. The only sound that could be heard was the TV of the neighboring patient and the machines that kept Ta'shauna Reed alive. With a bullet to the skull, the doctors had written her off as a goner, but miraculously she survived what should have been a fatal wound. Now she was in a fight, not one she faced with her fists, but one she would fight with her spirit and determination. After her surgery, the doctor said that it was out of his hands and it was all up to her now. If her will was strong enough then she could come out of her coma and make a full recovery. If it wasn't, then the Reeds would be making funeral arrangements.

When Threat had shot her in the head that day, he believed that was the end of her. There was one thing he wasn't counting on though. Her will to survive being stronger than her willingness to die. If Ta'shauna wasn't anything else, she was a fighter. She'd been chunking them all of her life. So it wasn't nothing for her to knuckle up and throw down for hers, but this was different. This was the greatest fight of her life against an opponent she'd never seen before, only heard about. It didn't matter though, because there wasn't any way in hell she was going out without a fight.

*Beep! Beep! Beep!* The heart monitor made its noise as a zig zag green line ran continuously across the screen. There was a stillness and then calmness inside of the room. And then a miracle happened, Ta'shauna's right hand twitched.

Lakita had just entered the room when she saw Ta'shauna's hand twitching. Frowning, she sat her clipboard down and stepped to her bed. She looked down at her hand waiting for it to move, but it didn't budge for quite some time. She reached down and caressed her arm, watching her fingers all the while.

"Come on, baby, come on." She tried to will her to move. Since she'd been Ta'shauna's nurse, every night when she came into work, she would talk to her as if she was aware and moving around. "Come on, Shauna, move that hand for me, pretty girl." She grasped her arm and stared at her hand. It seemed like a century had past, but finally it happened, her hand twitched.

"Ooooh!" Lakita cupped her hands to her face and jumped, as if something had scared her. Her eyes misted with tears and attempted to fall from her eyes. "Oh, my Jesus, it's a miracle! Dr. Charleston!" She mad dashed out of the hospital room thinking, *God is good, praise the Lord!*

***

When Chevy came from Kantrell's house she was defeated. Head hung and shoulders slumped, she entered her bedroom and gathered her under garments for a shower. She sat her underwear on the toilet seat and stepped into the medicine cabinet's mirror, looking herself over. Her face, as well as her clothes, were covered in dirt smudges. She peeled off her clothes, letting them fall in a pile at her bare feet. The last to go was her bra. As soon as she unlatched it, it dropped behind her. As naked as the day she entered this cold world, she placed her hands on the sides of the sink and stared into her reflection. Her eyes were red webbed and glassy with bags hanging underneath them. This, coupled with the harsh lights, made her look old and drained, something like a heroin addict that had been in the streets for a time. She looked like hell. Shit, she felt like it, too. The night she'd had was one she'd never forget, and with all that had occurred, how could she?

Finding out that her best friend had been fucking not only the man she'd fallen in love with, but her ex was a tremendous blow to her self esteem and ego. She didn't understand why she could never get it right with somebody. What was so wrong with her that one man couldn't be satisfied with being with just her?

She watched her eyes mist and bottom lip poke out. She sniffled and her vision blurred. Her shoulders shuddered and the tears streamed down her cheeks, trickling down into the porcelain sink. Her head dropped and when she looked back up, she found snot threatening to drip. Sniffling again, she wiped her face and nose with the back of her hand, slicking it.

"Ahhhhh!" She tilted her head back and screamed aloud, releasing all of that hurt and frustration. Suddenly, her head shot down and her clenched fist flew forward into the medicine cabinet's mirror. *Crack!* The glass cracked into a spider's web around her fist. Blood seeped from the cuts in her knuckles and soaked into the cracks and crevasses, outlining the breaks in the mirror. Slowly, she took her fist from the mirror and glass fell into the sink. Staring at her bloody knuckles, she went about the task of cleaning her wound and wrapping her hand up in an Ace bandage.

Chevy couldn't believe she'd been burned again by yet another man. No matter how many times she thought that she got it right, she didn't. She didn't understand how in the fuck could she constantly keep picking the wrong dudes? No one could have convinced her that Tiaz wasn't the right one for her. She could feel his love. When he talked, when her cell rang and his name was on the screen, when she felt his touch, the world stopped spinning. And in that moment, that instant, the lights dimmed and all she could see was *him*. What she believed was her Prince Charming was nothing more than a fucking toad dressed up in a snazzy suit. *Goddamn, all of these niggaz are the same,* she thought, shaking her head. She and Tiaz were through. She wasn't ever fucking with that nigga again. The chances of them being together died the moment he stuck his dick inside of her best friend. That was it. She'd made up her mind. She'd had enough with thugs. She was done with them!

Chevy closed her eyes and allowed her thoughts to roam. They came across Kantrell and instantly her face contorted with agitation. The thought of her made her sick to her stomach. She literally wanted to vomit. She hated everything about her. Her disloyalty was devastating. It rocked her world and strangled her heart. She didn't know if she'd ever let someone get so close to her again. Growing up, her mother had warned her to never allow another woman to get too comfortable around her man, because she'd surely steal him. It didn't even matter if the women weren't as attractive as her, leaving them alone with her man was a no no.

Back then she thought her mother was being over the top. She didn't think she'd ever have that to worry about. That was until now.

Chevy was told that no matter how much a man seemed content with his relationship that he was sure to roam in search of greener pastures. *Old pussy was good and familiar, but new pussy was foreign and intriguing,* her mother would say. This was just one of the many jewels she'd handed down to her when she was a kid. Oh, how she wished she would have devoured the lesson, because if she had then she wouldn't be feeling the sting of her lover's betrayal now. Chevy's bottom lip quivered and her eyes began to warm all over again. She could feel the tears coming, but she forced them back. She wouldn't allow tears to escape down her cheeks again. Her time of sadness had come and gone. She was done with grieving. She was going to focus all of her attention on raising her son and becoming a better her.

"It's okay," she counseled herself. "It's alright, small thang to a giant." She tried to convince herself.

Chevy shampooed and washed up under the spray of the showerhead, the hot water poured over her body. She stepped out and dried off thoroughly. After she got dressed for bed, she slid under the covers and killed the lamp light on the nightstand. Hearing a knock at her door, she turned over wearing a pair of baggy red rimmed eyes. She cleared her throat before she spoke.

"Come in." The knob clicked as it was turned and the door swung open, sending a ray of light through the darkened bedroom. A short silhouette stood in the doorway, the illumination from the hallway shining at its back. She snatched her Taurus .9mm from under the pillow, in fear for her life. She narrowed her eyes and peered closely, gripping her gun tighter.

"Mom, are you okay?" Te'Qui asked, concerned.

"Momma's okay, baby, how'd you get in?" Realizing it was her baby boy, she put her gun away.

"My keys." He held up his keys, jiggling them.

"How you know I was here?"

"I couldn't sleep with all of Brice's snoring. I heard you when you pulled up." He told her. Baby Wicked's house was right next door to their's.

"Oh."

Seeing the look on her face, he narrowed his eyes, face scrunching up. "Mom, you sure you're all right?"

She shook her head no and pursed her lips. She then opened her arms, wanting the loving embrace of the only one that loved her unconditionally in this world. He took off running into her arms, locking his arms around her. She squeezed her eyelids shut when she tilted her head against his.

"It's gon' be all right, mom. I'm here now, okay?"

"Thank you, baby, you're all momma needs." She meant it with every inch of her heart.

*\*\*\**

*Crack! Wop! Bap! Bwap!*

His head whipped from left to right before it hung. His bare, hairy chest inflated and deflated as he breathed. His face was swollen so badly that he looked like something out of a freak show. His face and chest were sweaty and slick with his blood. His feet had webbed and looked like those of a duck having had acid poured on them. He couldn't feel anything from the waist down having sat on the iron chair for the past couple of days. He'd been beaten to a pulp, stabbed in his nut sack with ice picks, set on fire and shot in the kneecaps with a nail gun. There wasn't an inch of him that didn't ache. His legs trembled uncontrollably, like it was thirty below outside. He was as frightened as a cornered mouse, not knowing what to expect as he peered out through his one good eye.

"Bitch made ass nigga!" One of the three thugs cracked his knuckles.

"Fucking sellout!" Another one shook his head, twisting his lips. He shook the pain in his hand he felt from punching on the capture.

"Y'all niggaz fall back. I'm finna put the weed wacker to this tall, skinny bastard." A third thug stepped forth, yanking the drawstring on the weed wacker. It kicked twice and roared to life, humming as the end of it spun around rapidly creating a white blur. Limb woke up. Hearing the noisy tool, he snapped his head all the way to the right as the weed wacker neared his face. The thug smiled maniacally, getting a kick out of the fear in his eyes. His jeans darkened at the crotch and wetness expanded, piss rolling off the edge of the chair and raining between his feet. He jerked around violently from left to right, moving his head up, down and all around, not wanting to experience the excruciation that the weed wacker was sure to bring.

*Doom! Doom! Doom!* The knocks at the large black iron door resonated throughout the warehouse. One of the thugs opened it and a man came strolling inside. All eyes were on him as he removed his hat and tossed it on a nearby table. En route to the capture, he snagged a chair and planted it in front of him. He removed his cape, draped it around the back of the chair and sat down, bringing a hand down his face as he exhaled. Leaning forward, he interlocked his fingers, peering into the captured man's face.

"You're a treacherous piece of shit, you know that?" Majestic started off. He was speaking of Limb giving Tiaz and Threat the info on the routes he took to get his money from his traps.

"Majestic, man, I…"

Majestic squeezed his eyelids closed. His nostrils flared and he gritted, holding up a finger.

"Don't you say it. Don't you fucking say it, you mothafucka you!" He looked like he was trying his damndest to keep from going off in a rage. The man looked scared as shit. His good eye was bugged and his teeth were chattering as his legs were shaking wildly.

The kingpin stood up and pushed the chair aside with his Mauri gator. "You betrayed us, and now you must be punished for your disloyalty." He kept his eyes on the bound man as he reached for the weed wacker. When he received it, he turned it back on. He stalked toward him with the end of the weed wacker spinning in a blur. The capture snapped his head back and forth, trying to avoid the onslaught of the tool.

"No. Nooo! Nooooo!" His glassy eye snapped open. He threw his head back and screamed at the top of his lungs, causing his uvula to shake. Veins bulged up his neck and temples.

Majestic stopped where he was and stuck the weed wacker in his face. He closed his eyes and turned his head as blood splattered on him, silencing the man for all eternity.

# Chapter Three
## *The next day*

*Smack!*

"Toot that ass up for me!" Tiaz ordered Kantrell.

"Mmmmm." She moaned softly when his palm came across her bodacious ass, causing it to jiggle. The assault left a red hand impression behind and she could feel its lingering sting. She hissed and arched her back as he slid the head of his dick into her slickened entrance. He sucked on his thumb and stuck it into her asshole and pursed his lips, letting hot saliva ooze and fall in a stream, pitter pattering his meat. He then began humping her, slowly at first, but then faster, enjoying her sensual moaning as he held one of her chunky cheeks apart with one hand and continued his stroking. He pushed and pulled himself out of her, throwing his head back and sucking his teeth. Her pussy was driving him mad. Her heat engulfed his dick, mound, and was working its way up his chiseled torso. They were almost as one as they went at it, both of their bodies moving united and working to bring them both to a blissfulness that could only be imagined.

"Ssssss," she hissed, eyes closed and mouth quivering as he hit that secret spot that would have her gushing. "That's it, don't stop, baby! I feel. I feel that shit," she whimpered, as he gave her those powerful thrust that showed off the toned muscles in his slightly hairy legs and hips. His beautifully sculpted thick veined dick sliding in and out of her warm, gooey tunnel caused it to spill her hot juices.

"What's that shit you feel, baby? Huh, tell Big Daddy what chu feel." He talked that shit as he pulled her hair back in a ponytail and held it tightly with both hands. Gritting his teeth, he showcased the bone structure in his jaws. As he peered down at his dick, watching it being gobbled up by that wet twat of hers, he punished that shit from the back, throwing that thang rapidly and make her spew more of her liquid. He gritted his teeth tighter, wrinkling his face further, and listened to the slapping of their dampened flesh as he pounded away, pulling her head back even further to expose her throat. He sunk his teeth into her neck gently and began to suck on it, like a blood thirsty vampire. Her eyes rolled up and her shoulders hunched back and forth.

"Mmmmm." He made the noise like he was sucking on a ripe, juicy peach. The entire time he kept up the pace of the dick he was giving her. He gave her the dick like those Columbian niggaz gave D-boys their dope, raw and uncut. As he licked up her neck then pulled back, a thin line of saliva came with him, which he wiped off and used to lubricate two of his fingers. He massaged that delicate nub of meat that dwelled between her fat coochie lips as he pummeled her from the back, causing a ripple to sweep up her healthy buttocks.

"Ah, fuck, ah shit." She sunk her fingers into the silk sheet and pulled them into her palm. Her face contorted and her toes curled like fried shrimp. He was dicking that ass down good, real good. She was sure that he was going to be her best fuck ever.

"Uh huh." He licked his sweaty lips as perspiration dripped from his brow. "What I tell yo' ass? What I tell you, nigga?" He smacked her ass violently, causing her to frown and whine. Yeah, it hurt, it hurt so mothafucking good.

"You hear me talking to you, huh?"

*Smack!* Another violent smack to her rear and she cried in ecstasy.

"You was gon' fuck the shit outta me!"

"What? Speak the fuck up!" He grabbed both of her ass cheeks and spread those thangs apart. His tongue hung out of his mouth as he watched his dick jab her middle hurriedly. He grunted and grunted, feeling his meat swell as he was about to bust.

"You was gon' fuck the shit outta meeeeeeeee!" She crooned like Patti Labelle before catching the Big O and falling face first into the mattress with her ass still hiked up.

"Yeah, yeah, yeah, I'm killing this mothafuckin' pussy." He looked from her to his cock, which he was still plunging in and out of her cunt. "Fuck Tiaz, call me P.K., baby, The Pussy Killah!" He relished in his moment of glory knowing he had thoroughly satisfied his fuck partner. Turning to the side, he planted his bare foot against the side of her head and sped up, humping the shit out of her. She'd already gotten off, so he was free to go ahead and get his off.

"What's my name?" he grumbled and smacked her ass, causing her to grimace. "I said, what's my name?" *Smack!*

"The Pussy Killahhhh!" she called out wincing, face melting back to one of pleasure.

"Don't chu ever forget it, either." His thick fingers sunk into her meaty ass, making impressions. His hot sweat pelted her cheeks as he grunted and worked her center, moving his hips as if he was a male stripper, grinding all up in that mothafucking pussy. Seeing the veins bulge in his member, he whipped it out at the last possible second.

She licked her top lip and revealed the small metal ball that was her tongue ring. Her tongue circled her top lip and went under her bottom before slithering back inside of her mouth. She shook that big old ass of hers as he jacked his meat, wrinkling it and straightening it as he did so. His lips trembled and then they came apart, putting his clenched teeth on display.

"Arghhh!" he snarled, his warm spunk shot out of the head of his one eyed snake, tatting up her ass cheeks and back. He continued to jerk himself until he was sure he had released every last drop. Relief crossed his face and he laid his slightly erect dick between her ass crack. He grinned as he watched her slide her crack up and down his deflated dick. He then smacked her buttocks one last time before climbing out of bed.

"I don't wanna hear any more about this killing Chevy business, ya understand me?" He pointed a finger.

"Yes, daddy." She grinned and nodded.

"Alright now."

Tiaz moved around the bedroom gathering underwear and the items he'd need to take a shower. He'd just thrown a towel over his shoulder and was heading toward the bathroom door when Kantrell called him back. He turned around with an eyebrow raised like *What's up with it?*

"You about to take a shower?" she asked in a funny voice, holding smoke in her lungs. He nodded and she mashed the cigarette she'd lit out into the ashtray. "I'ma join you."

"Nah, I need you to make that move for me."

"What move?" Her forehead wrinkled.

"I needa couple masks and some jumpsuits."

"Alright. Well, gimmie the money." She flexed her fingers greedily.

Tiaz picked his Dickies up from off the floor and reached inside one of the pockets. He pulled out a thick wad of dead presidents. He licked his thumb and counted off a few hundred dollar bills, tossing them on the bed beside her. She picked the money up and began straightening it out and counting it. Once she was done, she looked up at him and signaled him over with the coiling of her manicured finger. She smiled sexily as he approached, looking up at him and puckering up her lips. He smirked and leaned forward, planted his fists into the bed. He kissed her long and sloppily. The saliva could be heard squishing around in their mouths.

They'd just had mind blowing sex and their betrayal of Chevy was the farthest thing from their minds.

\*\*\*

Chevy hung the silhouette sheet up and pressed a button, sending it as far back as she could, then adjusted her protective goggles and protective ear wear. She extended the .9mm Taurus before her, tilted her head slightly as she took aim and pulled the trigger. The gun recoiled as it spat fire, tearing holes through the heart of the silhouette sheet and then the head. She always took it to the gun range to release some steam and burn off her frustration.

Inside of her mind, she imagined herself kicking in her bedroom door to find her best friend and her men sexing. She watched them scream in horror as she unloaded on them.

Chevy lowered her gun at her side and held down the button that would send the sheet back to her. Once she'd gotten it back in her possession, she examined it thoroughly, pleased with her handiwork.

"I'ma let this shit go. Yeah." She nodded in agreeance. "I'ma let it all go and move on with my life. I'ma stop letting these two trifling asses consume so much of my mind. You wanted him? Well you can have 'em, *bestie,* 'cause I'm through. I'll let karma settle this one up."

It had only been a few days, but she missed Tiaz. She knew she shouldn't miss him after finding out about his betrayal, but she couldn't help herself. It was that damn heart of hers. She had a habit of falling for the wrong type of men. Even when her conscience told her to steer clear of certain types of dudes, she'd ignore it. She figured it was because she wanted to fall in love and live happily ever after, like the girls in Walt Disney animated movies. She knew she was silly for thinking that way. This wasn't some cartoon, this was real life.

Tiaz had been blowing her phone up since that night they'd buried Azule's body. More than once she found herself about to answer, but then she'd think about it. He'd cheated on her just as Faison did. He didn't give a fuck about hurting her, so he didn't deserve the love she had to give. She refused to sweep what he had done under the rug. There was no way that she was going to get back with him and turn a blind eye to him cheating on her. She wasn't a weak bitch, she was a queen in her own right and deserved to be treated as such. One day she'd meet the man that was tailored made for her, she just knew it. Until then she'd wait for him.

### *Later that night*
"You sure that's the truck?" Tiaz asked as he drove a safe distance from a white Dodge Durango in a stolen Pontiac Grand Prix. It was the middle of the night, so the streets were scarce with vehicles.

"Positive." Threat looked from the photo of an identical truck then to the one that they were tailing. "Now where the hell is Don's bitch ass at?" He surveyed their surroundings. They were going to take the money and the dope and leave the Trap God staring up into the sky, chest looking like a used Maxi pad. The Durango transported the dead presidents while Don's whip would have the cargo, which was the coke.

"He'll turn up. We just gotta play it cool."

Hearing a pattering foot against the floor of the G-ride, Tiaz looked to find Threat impatiently tapping his foot. The expression he wore was one of great agitation. He always got like that. He wanted things to happen right there and right *now*!

"Where you think he's holding that bag at?" Threat looked to his crime partner.

"Typical place." Tiaz looked to Threat's hands. He was locking and loading the MP-5. His brows furrowed. He worried that Threat's impatience and temper would land them in some unnecessary mess they might not be able to get out of. "What chu doing?"

"We're taking 'em!" He pulled a clown mask over his face.

"Nigga, what?" He grabbed his arm.

"I said, we're taking 'em, nigga, get on yo' shit!" He yanked his arm away.

"What about Don?"

"Don can eat a dick!"

"Fuck!" Tiaz pulled a clown mask of his own down over his face. His gloved hand gripped the steering wheel and the other pulled his MP-5 over into his lap.

"Slide up on that mothafucka, Crim!" Threat scanned the area for The Ones before oozing out of the window and sitting on the windowsill. While he took his place, Tiaz eased alongside the speeding Durango, looking back and forth between it and the windshield.

"Speed up, nigga, and swing up in front of it!" The shorter killer barked, clutching that big black mothafucka with both hands. His trigger finger was itching like it had poison ivy, begging to get its exercise in for the night.

Tiaz floored it and swung out in front of the vehicle that they were pursuing, cutting it off. Threat brought his machine gun up and around the roof of the car. When the eyes of the dreadlock rocking driver of the SUV met with the barrel of the lethal weapon, they snapped open. His mouth formed the letter O and his cigarette dropped in his lap. The little man squeezed the trigger of his MP-5. It rattled to life in his hands, bucking wildly and spitting fire, tattering the windshield. Holes blew through the glass creating several spider web cracks. Burgundy splatters smacked up against the ruined windshield. The truck swerved out of control and slammed into a light post.

Tiaz pulled the getaway car up beside the wrecked vehicle. He left the engine running, his gloved hands grabbed his machine gun and he hopped out. Threat jumped down from out of the window and followed his partner in crime, approaching the Durango with caution. Tiaz opened the driver's door and pulled the dead body from behind the wheel, letting it fall to the asphalt. He popped the locks. Once he and his right hand moved to the backseat, he drew a machete, stabbed it into the leather seat and dragged it. He sheathed the blade and tore open the split he'd made. His eyes lit up when he saw the Benjamin Franklins wrapped in plastic. He and his crime partner whistled, slapping each other high five.

They pulled duffle bags from around their backs and began loading bricks of money into them. Before they could finish they were blinded by bright headlights from both ends. They hopped out of the truck and looked around. They were being boxed in by two black H2 Hummers. The doors of the beasts swung open and a total of four dreadlock wearing men emerged, Uzis ready to shoot to death.

*Ping! Ting! Zing!*

Tiaz bobbed and weaved the heat rocks as they were spat his way. He ducked down and crawled beneath the Durango, sweeping his machine gun back and forth. Arghhh! Gaahhh! Two of the dreads fell out, the sides of their faces hitting the cool street, faces grimacing in agony. They hollered out for God and Tiaz sent them to meet him with a second sweep of his weapon.

Threat threw the SUV into reverse and allowed it to roll back. He rounded the vehicle, taking shots at the remaining dreads, mangling one of their heads and necks before advancing on the other one. The other man was hunched over and running around the back of the other car. He ran and threw himself over the hood of the truck, landing on his feet with the agility of a cat. Peeking underneath the Durango, he saw his targets ankles as he moved to get the drop on him. He pointed that thang at him and blew his legs out from underneath him. When his dome met the ground he hollered out, stretching open his mouth. Threat sent a couple into the gaping hole, splattering his brains out the back of his skull. The SUV crashed into the Hummer and he approached him, pointing his weapon at him, he sprayed his ass. *Blaaaaaaaaaat! Road kill!*

Threat fished a cell phone out of the corpse's pocket and snapped pictures of the carnage they'd created. He then punched in Don Juan's number and sent it to him in a picture text. Afterwards, he threw the cell phone aside.

Hearing the police sirens hastily approaching, the crime partners stuffed the last of the money into their duffle bags and hauled ass back to the G-ride. They slammed the doors of the vehicle shut and peeled off.

Later that night, Tiaz and Threat split the take they made from the hit, seventy-five thousand dollars apiece. The risk was well worth it.

Bury Me A G 2

# Chapter Four
## *A week later*

Tiaz sat back on the couch staring at his cell phone. There was a picture on the screen of he and Chevy from the night they spent at the club.

*Damn, Chev, I know a nigga fucked up, boo. I broke yo' heart and proved to you that I'm no better than the rest of them niggaz that shitted on you.* He shook his head. *A mothafucka sorry though, real shit, Love. It's true what they say, 'you don't realize what you have until it's gone.' So true, oh so fucking true. I guess it's really over between us. I can't blame nobody but myself, though. It's my fault.*

Since she had thrown him out of the house, he'd been shacking up with Kantrell. Kantrell was cool and all, but she for damn sure wasn't clean. Her house was a pigsty. It looked like a tornado had been through that mothafucka. On top of that, she couldn't cook for shit. Her refrigerator was loaded with microwavable TV dinners. She didn't iron his clothes, draw his baths, give him massages, or TiVo his favorite shows when she knew that he'd be out in the streets late. He'd gotten fed up with Kantrell's way of living, so he rented a place of his own, a three bedroom house out in Compton.

Tiaz felt that he could never be the man that Chevy wanted him to be. He recognized this while he was incarcerated, but he still wanted her to be his, so pretended to be what she was looking for. He figured once he'd gotten in good enough that he could slowly ease her into his old lifestyle and she'd accept it. If he saw any resistance then he'd continue to live his lie.

Tiaz didn't see himself settling down with a wife and kids anytime soon. He had money on his mind and he was trying to get plenty of it before the pearly gates opened or a fiery pit was ignited for him, whichever came first. Chevy wanted a hard working nine to five brother that she could come home to at night. She wanted someone to settle down and grow old with, and he just wasn't that type of guy. He was being realistic with himself. He was a thug ass nigga that got his by any means necessary. He lived fast and was poised to die young. With his lifestyle, he knew that death was around the corner and he was all right with that, as long as he got to live it up before his time came.

Tiaz pushed the thoughts of Chevy to the back of his mind. He had to get his head right if he was going to pull off this next caper, so until he was done with this next job, Chevy, Te'Qui and everyone else would be as good as dead to him.

"Who are you texting, nigga?" Threat asked Tiaz as he handed him a Heineken.

"This fool that owe me some bread, nigga got an excuse every time it comes time to pay. I may have to smack'em upside the head with that thang so he can get his mind right, nah what I'm saying?" he lied, staring his right hand in his eyes as he removed the cap from his Heineken.

"Shit, if you want we can swing by and see that nigga," Threat said from the love seat where he sat taking swigs from a beer.

"It's all good. I'ma handle it."

There was a knock at the door. Threat took a peek through the curtains. Once he saw who it was, he opened the door and stepped aside. Kantrell walked in with a black bag of items. Her face was still bruised and scarred from the fight with Chevy, but it had healed considerably. Threat closed the door behind her as she went inside of the kitchen.

Tiaz took a swallow of his beer and sat it on the coffee table. He then headed into the kitchen, kissed Kantrell, then watched Threat reach into the black bag and pull out three taser guns, one by one. He picked up one and so did Threat. They examined the taser guns and checked their sightings.

"Where did you get these from?" Tiaz asked Kantrell as he aimed the taser gun at something across the kitchen.

"At the surplus over on Hawthorne Boulevard."

"You didn't go inside and pay for this yourself, did you?"

"Nah, I paid a smoker to go in for me. I know better than that."

"That's my bitch." Tiaz smacked her on the ass, she stopped and made it clap, licking her tongue at him. "Gimme a kiss." She leaned closer, kissing him.

"You think this will be enough to drop fat boy?" Threat asked Tiaz.

"Man, once all of that juice shoots through that nigga, his big ass gone fold like a fuck nigga under questioning," Tiaz assured.

"Look!" Threat's forehead wrinkled as he pointed at the flat-screen. Tiaz and Kantrell turned around to see what he was talking about. There was a breaking news report on Channel 5 about the discovery of Limb's dead body, a picture of Limb, his girlfriend and their two children was on the screen.

"Threat, turn it up," Tiaz said.

Threat picked up the remote control and turned up the volume.

*Daniel 'Limb' Stokes' body was discovered in a grassy field in the back of an abandoned Mattel toy factory in The City of Industry. He was found with his wrists bound behind his back and his throat slit. 'Judas' was carved into his forehead. If you have any information that may help the local police solve this case, we urge you to call 1-800...*

Threat turned the flat screen off and sat the remote control down beside him. "We've got to find this mothafucka, man, 'cause he's for damn sure looking for us."

"How in the hell are we gone find'em? We've been looking all over the city for this old ass nigga. No one knows where he stays or any places that he frequents. He's been like a ghost since that night at the club. Cat just up and vanished in the air."

"Let's just focus on snatching this nigga up for this check and then we'll focus on smoking grandpa. He's bound to have some family around somewhere. We can snatch'em up and make his old ass come to us."

\*\*\*

Day Day hung from a meat hook inside of a restaurant freezer, getting a beating that hadn't been seen since the *Passion of the Christ* movie. Bone stood behind him gripping a cat-o-nine tails with talons at the ends of it, twirling it above his head. He drew his hand back and brought it down the young man's back, slicing up the flesh of his hide and leaving bleeding gashes behind. Day Day hollered in agony, but his cries were muffled by the black ball gag plugging his mouth. Each time he was assaulted by the object of torture, he danced at the end of the hook. Faison watched the torture while drinking a glass of Cognac, seeming not the slightest bit disturbed by the scene playing out before him. He didn't find any pleasure in watching the young man being ravaged, but it was a necessary evil. He believed that he had some very valuable information that he needed and he was willing to do anything within his means to obtain it.

Bone drew the cat-o-nine tails back and brought it down the youth's back one last time. Droplets of blood dripped upon the cold floor of the freezer, causing vapors to rise. Faison stepped back to avoid specs of blood from hitting his Versace loafers. Bone brought the hand that he held his weapon with to his side. His chest heaved up and down as he wiped the beads of sweats from his forehead with the back of his hand. Bird looked to Faison and he gave him a nod. He then removed the ball gag from the young man's mouth. He held the boy's head up and he groaned in pain, his eyes were rolled to their whites.

"Aye, aye." Bird smacked Day Day across the face twice, bringing him to.

"Who shot Ta'shauna Reed? Tell us what we wanna know, if you wanna get outta here."

"I don't know. I don't know." He whimpered then sobbed. Green snot oozed from out of his nose and drool ran from the corner of his mouth. "I swear to God, I don't know!"

Day Day was a little nigga in the hood that knew too much for his own good. If it went down or it was about to go down, then chances were he knew about it. He made his living dealing in information. He had knowledge of some of everyone's business, which is why he was hanging up in the freezer and getting the beating of his young life.

Faison grasped Bird's shoulder and he looked to him. He gave the youth the signal to step aside and he obliged. Faison walked around the suspended Day Day until he reached his back. He took another sip from his glass of Cognac, savored the taste and then splashed it onto the bloody gashes of his back.

"Arghhhhh!" He released a blood curdling scream with his eyelids squeezed closed, trembling at the end of the hook.

Faison scowled and threw his glass into the wall of the freezer, shattering it into pieces. He walked around so that the kid could see his face. Seeing the evil in the husky man's eyes caused a chill to slither up the young man's spine.

"I swear to God, man! I don't know who shot her!" Day Day wept. "I haven't heard anything, or I would have told you! That's on my momma, Faison! You've gotta believe me!"

"Now some niggaz deal in dope, some niggaz deal in pussy, but chu deal in information," Faison barked. "You know about some of everything that goes on in the streets, and you expect me to believe you don't know jack shit about the cat that popped my sister? Come on now, I know you got something for me to go on, a lil' piece of something." He showed the size with his fingers. "Whatever you got, I'll run with it. I just need a line on this cat, fam."

There was a momentary silence. The young man shook his head no. "I don't know anything, man! If I did, don't you think I would have spilled my guts by now? You got me hanging up in a fucking freezer like a slab of beef."

Faison hung his head and massaged the bridge of his nose. He'd become frustrated trying to find leads on Ta'shauna's shooter. He was starting to believe that either no one really knew anything or that they were keeping tight lipped about it. He thought the young man would have some information that would lead him straight to his sister's assailant, but he ended up hitting a road block with him. His cell phone rang and he answered it.

"Ma, gimme a second." He placed his hand over the receiver so his mother wouldn't hear what he was about to say. He whispered something into Bird's ear before heading out of the freezer. "What's going on, ma?" he asked, at that moment he heard the faint sound of a gunshot. His eyes bugged. Not from the sound of the gunshot, but from what his mother had just told him. "Alright, I'm on my way!" he disconnected the call and ran off.

***

Faison ran through the west wing hallway of Cedar Sinai Hospital. He almost knocked over a doctor and an old man coming out of his room pushing an IV pole. The nurse at the station yelled out to him that there was "no running in the hall," but he ignored her and continued his dash to Ta'shauna's room. Bending the corner at the end of the hall, he saw his mother and father outside of the waiting room door. Faison slowed his running to a stride before approaching them, breathing heavily.

"She's okay, she's gonna be all right," Gloria told her son with teary eyes. "She's going to be blind for the rest of her days, but the Lord was merciful. He let my baby keep her life." She embraced her only son, crying into the breast of his jacket.

"Is she awake?"

"Yes, but she can't talk, her throat is sore from the breathing tube."

Gloria moved aside and Faison Sr. approached his son, fidgeting with his hat. "Son, I think it's time that we sit down and..." before Faison Sr. could finish, his son moved passed him and headed toward his sister's room.

Seeing the hurt in her husband's eyes, Gloria caressed the side of his face. "He'll come around, sweetheart, just give'em a little time." Faison Sr. nodded and put his hat back on his crown. He and Gloria walked back into the waiting room.

When Faison entered Ta'shauna's room, he found her laid up like she was before, but this time she was breathing with the help of a nasal cannula.

"T, it's me, Faison, big bro." Her eyes looked to him, she tried to speak, but her throat was too sore from the breathing tube to form words. "Shhh, don't try to talk." He pushed a chair up to her bed and sat down, taking her hand into his.

"Did you hear me talking to you while you were in a coma?" he asked his sister. She nodded yes. "So you know Orlando didn't make it?" Her eyes welled up and she closed them. Tears shot down her cheeks. She opened them and nodded. "You know I wasn't his biggest fan, but I wouldn't wish death on anyone. Do you know who it was that clapped y'all up that day?"

She shook her head no. Faison thought on it for a moment. "Is there anyone you could think of that would send a hitter at you and Orlando?" She nodded yes. "Who? Do you know his name?" Her eyes darted back and forth to her hand, which he was holding in his own. He turned her wrist over and saw *Tiaz* tattooed in small cursive letters. His eyes bugged. *Ta'shauna's Tiaz couldn't be Chevy's Tiaz, and if he was then the world was truly a small place.*

"T, is Tiaz about six foot one, pecan brown, big muscles, rocks his hair in a fade?" She nodded her head. "Son of a bitch has been under my nose the whole fucking time," Faison said to himself, his face contorting into a mask of hatred. He already wanted Tiaz dead for taking his family away from him, now his reasoning was even stronger. At first he was going to let Bird and Bone get him out of his hair, but now he was going to make sure he was the one to push the thug into the afterlife.

"I'ma make sure this nigga pay for what he's done to you, sis. Big bro is going to take care of it, I got chu." He kissed her hand and patted it, then laid it back down on the bed and made his exit.

The elevator doors parted and Faison stepped out heading for the automatic double doors of the lobby exit. He pulled out his cell phone and punched in a number. He held the cell phone to his ear, listening as it rung. Finally someone picked up. "Aye, I need you to round up the goons and strap up. I know who did that thang. Yeah, y'all meet me at the spot." He hung up the cell phone and placed it back on his hip. As he walked through the automatic double doors and the fresh air of the outside rushed him, he felt the cool breeze through his twisties and the flapping of his coat's collar against his chin as he made his way towards the curb. Just as he was about to step down into the street, a limousine came to a screeching halt before him.

"Hey, watch where the fuck you going!" Faison kicked the passenger side back door.

The back window slowly rolled down and exposed the passenger. The passenger stared at Faison through the dark lenses of his shades. He put fire to his black pipe and sucked on the end of it. He held the smoke hostage in his lungs for a moment then blew it out into his face. Faison's face twisted into a scowl and he fanned the white smoke away from him.

"Hop in," the passenger ordered.

"I got somewhere to be, I'll get up with chu later."

"This isn't a request, nigga, get cho black ass in the car." The passenger stated firmly. His voice was calm, yet demanding, with a sense of authority to it.

Faison gave the man a look that read as *Fuck you think you are?* He made to leave and the driver side door swung open. A baldheaded man wearing a thick beard hopped out, reaching inside of his suit. Faison went to draw his banger, but the baldheaded man was quicker on the draw. He approached Faison, taking a cautious scan of his surroundings. He threw him up against the side of the limousine and swept his legs apart with his foot, patted him down and relieved him of his banger. As he opened up the back door, he tucked the banger on his waistline then deposited him inside, like he was a criminal being put into the back of a police cruiser.

"TJ, meet Faison, Faison meet TJ, my nephew." The passenger introduced the young cat sitting beside him in a white T-shirt and tan Dickie shorts. His socks were pulled up to his knees and he was wearing low-top All-Star Chuck Taylor Converses. Beside him rested a couple of forearm crutches. He was a frizzy cornrow wearing dude with a pecan hue. He looked up from the blunt he was rolling and gave Faison a nod. Faison returned the gesture.

"This must be serious, you kidnapping me and shit," Faison said.

"You bet your ass," the passenger poured him a glass of Cognac and then himself a glass.

"What is it?" Faison asked, swirling the liquor around in his glass. He listened as the passenger gave him the rundown.
What he heard let him know that the world was truly a small place.

# Chapter Five

Kiana stood in front of the nightstand mirror straightening out the wrinkles in her peach colored scrubs uniform. Head angled from side to side, she took in her appearance with a smirk on her lips. She was a brown skinned girl with long wavy like hair that was passed down to her through her Dominican mother. Her dimpled cheeks and pair of thick sexy lips begged to be kissed. Kiana was a Licensed Vocational Nurse at UCLA Hospital. She'd met her first and last lover in middle school. He hugged the block to pay for his expensive tastes and her way through nursing school. The couple had been married for eleven years and were still very much in love.

After intertwining her fingers within a scrungy, she pulled her hair back into a ponytail and tangled it in it. She slipped on her nurse's badge and sprayed her neck and wrists with Bath & Body Works Beach Cabana. Just as she sat the bottle down, a pair of strong chocolate hands snaked their way around her waistline. A smile broadened her face when she saw her husband nestle his nose at the nape of her neck, placing soft kisses on it.

"You in here smelling good, looking good," he claimed. "I'm 'bout ready to bend you over and have my way with you."

She placed her hands on top of his and smiled, showcasing all thirty-two of her pearly white teeth, the dimples of her cheeks deepening.

"Uh uh, now see there, you always trying to get something started when I'm tryna get to work."

"It's all your fault, Lover."

"Oh really?" She raised an eyebrow.

"Yep." He continued kissing up her neck.

"How do you figure?"

"You shouldn't have gotten all pretty and shit," he replied.

"The blame is on you. I'm completely innocent." She laughed and giggled, staring at their reflection in the mirror.

"Gimme some lip." He told her and their mouths massaged one another while their tongues did a mating ritual. The kiss was a little wet, so when she pulled back she saw moisture on his top lip. She wiped it away with her thumb and pecked him twice. They stared into each other's eyes, but that special moment was quickly broken by...

Waa! Waa! Waa!

"Damn," Don Juan stood erect, tugging on his dick. He was good and hard. He looked into the crib and found the baby flailing his little arms and kicking.

"That reminds me, you're gonna have to drop him off at Tammy's."

"Tammy's?" He frowned. "Fuck happened to Rosa?"

She playfully smacked him on the cheek.

"Watch your mouth now," she ordered. "You know babies pick things up at a young age."

He cracked a smile and said, "Betta watch it, girl, you know yo' man likes it rough."

"I do too, but I don't have time, I'm gonna be late for work." She sat down on the bed, putting on her sneakers.

Don Juan dipped his hands into the crib and came back up with his offspring. He held him to his chest while gently patting his back.

"What's up with Rosa though?" He inquired about their babysitter and housekeeper.

"She had a doctor's appointment today." She slipped on her jacket and then grabbed her purse and lunch bag.

"Oh yeah, when will she be back?"

"Tomorrow."

"Smooth." He looked to his son and then to his wife. "Lil' man sleeping?"

"Yeah." She stole a peek.

"Alright. Let me walk you downstairs." He grabbed the baby's bottle as he disappeared through their bedroom door behind her.

When they made it downstairs he kissed her goodbye and closed the door behind her. As soon as the lock clicked, the baby started back up again.

Waa! Waa! Waa!

"Uh uh." Don Juan hushed his four month old son as he walked him around the dining room, rocking him gently as he tried to feed him his bottle. "What I tell you 'bout that crying, Junior? Yo' old man ain't raising no bitch. You betta calm that shit down." The baby took the nipple into his mouth and the whining stopped as he closed his eyes. "Yeeaahh, there we go, that's a big boy." He spoke to his child as he continued his journey around the dining room. Donovan Jr., or DJ as he was affectionately called, was a miracle baby. His umbilical cord was wrapped around his neck and he was blue in the face when he was cut from his mother womb. They'd pronounced the little guy dead, but then something happened. His fingers and toes began to twitch. His eyes fluttered open. He came alive, real animated like. Don and Kiana felt blessed that the Lord Almighty had saw it fit to spare their child. Unbeknownst to his wife, the kingpin had bartered a deal with God. If he allowed his baby boy to live, he'd keep the boy on a straight and narrow path, keeping his nose clean of the street life. He had big plans for junior, bright lights, jerseys and a pigskin football. He saw his boy as a big time athlete.

If there was anything Don Juan loved more than hustling it was being a dad. It brought him great joy and added meaning to his life.

He never smiled or laughed so much before Kiana had his seed. It was kind of funny, because the family man he displayed when he was with his relatives was a far cry from the merciless gangsta he was in the trenches. It was like when Clark Kent jumped inside of that phone booth and out flew Superman.

The ringing of the doorbell stole his attention and his head snapped in its direction. He asked who it was, but no one responded. With that in mind, he pulled his ratchet from the small of his back and proceeded toward the door with caution. After taking a gander from through the curtains, he put his tool up and opened the door. He stood aside allowing Juvie and Lil' Stan to enter. He stuck his head out of the sliding glass patio door and peered up and down the block, making sure his people weren't followed.

"Y'all handled that?" he asked them, steadily rocking the baby as he sucked on the bottle.

They nodded.

### An hour earlier

The day was warm with plenty of sunlight. It was 9:30 in the morning. The intersection between Florence and Hoover was exceptionally quiet, with the occasional car passing by, pedestrians moving about, and the street sweepers brushing up the loose trash alongside the curb. Suddenly, a triple black van pulled up at the intersection, nearly being hit by a semi as it had stopped the flow of traffic. Cars from all four of the paralleling streets honked their horns and shouted threats and insults.

The double doors of the van opened outward and a man dressed in a ski mask and black hooded sweat suit jumped out, holding twin black garbage bags which were pissing blood from the bottoms of them. One by one, he emptied the bags and severed body parts came tumbling out like loose shoes. Once he was finished, he threw the bags aside and jumped back inside of the van, pulling the double doors closed as it sped away in a hurry.

The occupants of the vehicles wore shocked expressions. Slowly, some of them began to emerge from their cars and approach the body parts that lay strewn at the intersection. They found two severed heads with horror etched across their faces. They both were wide eyed with their mouths stretched open. Carved into their foreheads was *disloyalty*. The occupants of the vehicles looked from the severed heads to up the block where all they could see were the back lights of the speeding van as it bent the corner. Its license plate was missing so they couldn't ID the vehicle. One of the onlookers vomited, while another one ran off with his hand covering his mouth to throw up.

"Someone call the cops!" one of the onlookers said.

A blur of a man shot passed him en route to the phone booth across the street.

### *Present*

"Yeah, we did that," Juvie answered from the couch, both arms stretched across the back of it.

"The streets gon' be talking about this one." Lil' Stan pulled out a cigarette and a lighter about to spark up.

"My nigga, do you or do you not see me with my fucking seed in here?" Don Juan's face twisted, projecting a dangerous look.

"My bad, Don, forgot chu gotcha lil' one in here and shit." He snatched the Joe out of his mouth and stashed the lighter in his pocket.

Juvie nudged Lil' Stan and gave him a disbelieving expression.

"Youz a stupid ass nigga."

"What? I said my bad. I forgot the homie had his son up in here." Lil' Stan shot back in a hushed tone, with his face balled up.

"Imbecile." Juvie spoke under his breath.

"Whatever, my nigga," Lil' Stan stated peevishly.

Don Juan sighed and shook his head, continuing his pacing around the dining room. "But yeah, that's exactly how I wanted this shit done, so everybody will be talking about it. Let the streets know that The Don ain't nothing to be fucked with. That right there, that play that y'all just laid down, was on some Mexican cartel type of shit. It'll show these lil' knuckleheaded mothafuckaz out here that disrespect, betrayal, disloyalty and snitching will not be tolerated, straight like that." Juvie and Lil' Stan nodded in agreement.

"So what's up, man? What're we gone do about Tiaz and Threat?" Juvie inquired. "The custies are starting to think that we're the ones setting them up. You know we can't have that, it's fucking up our paper."

"I've been getting death threats ever since that nigga Roots people got hit before they could make that pickup."

"You think it's his people?"

"With them funny ass accents, ain't nobody but them dreads."

"Tiaz, Threat, Roots and his people, fuck are we gon' do about these fools, fam?"

"What chu think we're gon' do?" Don Juan drew his gun and pointed it at him. "Pow! Pow!"

A crooked grin spread across Juvie's face and he nodded his approval. He lived for the drama. It made his dick hard.

### *Two days later*

A jovial expression appeared on Uma's face seeing the name on the letter that was sent to her. She was excited as a child on Christmas morning as she tore off the end of the envelope and pulled out the letter. Unfolding the letter, she slipped on her reading glasses and began reading over it. The joyous expression slowly began its retreat and a saddened look crossed her face, giving birth to a pair of sentimental eyes. Her eyes misted with tears and her bottom lip quivered uncontrollably.

"Oh ma Lord, ma baybe, ma baybe bwoi." Tears spilled from the corners of her eyes and her lips trembled as if they were in the blistering cold. She staggered back with her hand over her chest, falling out onto the floor, unconscious.

"Uduka, something is wrong with mommy." Uche told his brother, seeing his mother stagger and fall back on the floor. They dropped the goat that they had slaughtered and hustled towards the hut, their sandaled feet hurriedly making tracks. They took their spears in both hands as they neared their home, ready to shed the blood of anyone or anything that may have harmed their mother. The brothers slowed to a jog as they approached the hut. They stepped inside with their necks on a swivel and their weapons poised to do whatever posed a threat up really filthy.

"Uma," Uduka identified his mother and attended to her. She was lying sprawled about unconscious, her hand holding tight to the letter she'd gotten from her middle son. Uche kneeled down to his mother alongside his little brother. He took the letter from her hand as his sibling tried desperately to revive her, smacking her across the face. "Mommy, wake up, wake up, wake up." His ashy black hand gently smacked her cheek.

Uche's face balled up as he read over the letter. His eyes turned glassy and his mouth quivered as he gritted his teeth heatedly. "Grrrrr, uhhh." He stabbed his spear into the ground, stealing his little brother's attention. By this time their mother had slowly began coming to.

Worry lines etched across Uduka's forehead as he peered up at his big brother massaging the bridge of his nose.

"Uche, wat's da matta? Wat happened?" he questioned anxiously. Uche continued to massage his nose as he passed him the letter. He snatched the letter from him and quickly scanned over it. His face contorted into something ugly as hot tears stung his pupils and tears slicked his cheeks wet. A soft whimper left his lips, snapping his brother's head in his direction. His eyes were dark and soulless, while his lips formed a tight line. The look he projected took his little brother off guard. He looked like a tiger about to pounce on his prey. Startled, Uduka dropped the letter and hastily backed up on his hands and the balls of his feet, looking petrified. Uche was on him like stink on shit. He snatched him up and lifted him to his feet, smacking him across his face viciously.

*Smack! Smack! Smack!*

The assault left the little brother's cheeks stinging. The redness looked like blush makeup against his jet black skin. He blinked his eyes, looking at his sibling with fearful eyes. There wasn't a man standing on two feet that Uduka Eme was afraid of besides his brother. He'd rather go up against a pride of lions than face his wrath.

Uche stared up into his little brother's eyes with squared jaws that threatened to burst.

"Don't chu eva waste ya teahs crying for our brudda," he grumbled furiously. "You use your time ta shed blood for him, ya heah me, Duke?"

Uduka closed his eyes and took a deep breath, nodding his head rapidly. His big brother let him down to his feet, straightening out his collar and smoothening out his shirt. He then gripped him by the back of his neck, kissed his forehead and held his forehead against his.

Uche scooped up his mother and carried her over to the bed, lying her down. As he moved to make her comfortable he listened to Uduka.

"Wat are we going ta do now, Uche? Boxy is dead."

Boxy was the second oldest out of The Eme Brothers. He was sent to America to avoid persecution for murdering a man that tried to molest him. Unfortunately, the relatives that his family sent him to live with were crack heads on the low. They sold off all of his valuables to support their habits and when he went ham they kicked him out of the house. Leaving him an orphan and in the care of a surrogate mother. The streets.

"We go ta America and find his keela and bring him ta justice," he answered, draping a blanket over his mother. He was kissing her on the forehead when he heard him speak again.

"Ya mean da police?"

"Fuck da police!" He whipped around, eyebrows arched and nose scrunched. "He'll answer to us, his blood." He balled his ashy, callused hands into fists. His eyes were webbed red and glassy. He looked like a man that had gone mad.

"Right. He'll answer to us." Uduka's face took on the same terrifying look as his kin. He, too, thirsted for the blood of their sibling's executioner. "We'll need money ta get ta da states though."

"We can stow away onna ship. All we'll need is money ta cash in fa American dollas."

"Do ya have anything putta way?"

"Yes. But I'm sure it will not be enough," he told him. "We'll borrow da rest."

"Okay."

"Pack only ya necessities. We leave tonight." He laid down a button down shirt and began tossing the items he'd need for the trip.

"Alright." Uduka went to pack his things.

Night took the day hostage so the only thing to keep the village lit was the wafting fires of a dozen torches. The night was quiet, more quiet than usual. All that the natives felt permeated the air, their pain, their despair, their anguish. Their sadness and weeping was enough to soften the coldest heart of hearts. The village's people wore tear stained faces, having heard Uche tell them of his brother being murdered. All of them knew him since he was a little boy. They knew him as a very happy go lucky kid that loved to eat. They didn't have a clue to the ruthless thug he had become since moving to the United States.

"...So I ask ya ta give us wat eva little you have ta offa." Uche's eyes took in all of the grief stricken faces. *Okay, yes, we'll help you,* were just some of the words that were spoken before the villagers disassembled, going off to get what money they had or valuables that could be turned in to get American currency. By ones, by twos and by threes they returned, setting money and valuables at the brothers' feet. The men and women consoled the brothers with hugs, kisses, or manly condolences.

"Do ya ting dis a be enough fa ya journey?" Uma asked her oldest son as he thanked the people that approached for helping him fund the trip.

"I hope so. We're going ta need every dime." He answered right before embracing a grieving heavy set woman that was like an aunt to him and his brothers.

After the brothers thanked their neighbors, they took a sack each and started gathering the dollars and coins. They loaded the rest of the stuff inside of the flat-bed of an old, dull, burgundy and rusted pickup truck. They rode into town and cashed everything in.

Uche climbed inside of the truck and slammed the door shut with Uduka getting in right behind him. The young African peered over at his older sibling as he pulled knot after knot of money out of the velvet sack he'd stuffed the cash in from the exchange.

"How much?" he asked curiously.

"Shut up, you're gon' make me lose dee count." He paused and then got right back to counting up that paper. A smirk graced his lips as he counted the last of the dollars.

"Come on, come on, how much?" he asked anxiously, seeing him secure the money in bands and stash it back in the sack.

"Thirty thousand in U.S. currency."

"Wow."

"Hold dis." He passed him the sack. "Guard dat wit ya life." He resurrected the pickup and pulled off.

They came off with more than enough money they'd need for their stay in America and to send their brother back home to be buried. As soon as the brothers made it back home, they didn't waste any time gathering their things for the journey. They said their goodbyes to the people of their village, before bidding farewell to their mother.

"Dis was ya father's," she told Uche as she slipped a beaded necklace over his head. It was decorated with a lion's fangs, a bird's feathers, and a crocodile's eye. "It was passed down from his father and so on and so forth. I should have given it ta ya years ago, but there's no time like dee present." She turned to her youngest boy, taking his hand and extending it. She slipped a bracelet around his wrist that was made of black wooden beads and had a unique designed carved in it. "And dis was also ya father's. It was his good luck charm. He wore it every day except for the one he was killed on." She peered into his pupils with glassy, hurt filled eyes. She remember the day Timone was murdered like it was yesterday and would hate to revisit it if something were to happen to one of her sons.

"Please, please, please be careful," she told her son's, shaking her interlocked hands. "I cannot stress it enough."

"We will, mommy." Uche nodded, holding her hands, gazing into her eyes.

"Oh my." She broke down, hanging her head and sobbing. Tears outlined her eyelids and lashes, sliding down her cheeks. "Jesus, help me, Father." She placed a hand to her chest. Uche and Uduka placed a hand on her shoulders, looking at her with concern, foreheads creased. "I'm sorry, I'm sorry." She sniffled and stood upright, trying to pull herself together. "Come here, the both of you." They approached and she locked her arms around them, holding them tightly in her embrace. She closed her eyes and captured the moment inside of her head. She didn't want to forget it, in case they never made it back. She kissed them both on their cheeks.

"I love you both."

"We love you, too, mommy."

"Okay, once ya arrange for ya brudda ta be sent back, ya hurry home, okay?"

"Yes, mommy."

"Uduka," she cupped his face and kissed his forehead. "Ya listen ta ya brudda, he is da man of dis family. So wat he says goes, ya understand?"

He stole a glance at his big brother. Uche had the heart of a tiger and the ferociousness of a lion. He was the strongest of all of Timone and Uma's children. He was a natural born leader and just as brave as their father. Uduka felt secure knowing that his brother would be by his side. He looked from his sibling and settled his eyes back on his mother. "Yes, of course, mommy."

Staring into her youngest son's eyes, Uma's face contorted and her eyes welled. A tear rimmed her right eye and trickled down. She sniffled and wiped it with a curled finger. The African brethren exchanged concerned glances and attended to their mother.

"Mommy, wat is dee matta?" Uduka worried.

She shook her head, closed her eyes and took a deep breath, calming herself. "I'm fine bwois. Give ya mudda love." She mustered a halfhearted smile and her sons embraced her.

They gathered their things and started off walking. Their mother watched their back as they trekked off into the night, looking up into the ebony sky.

With her hands together in prayer, she said, "Please, God, watch over my baybees and bring them back home to me in one piece. I beg of you." Her voice cracked, oozing with emotion. Tears fled down her face, dripping down. "I beg of you, please."

That same night, Uche and Uduka snuck their way upon a ship and stashed themselves somewhere deep inside of its bowels. The space was dark and wet and they could hear all of the movement and voices above on deck.

"Pull 'em in and set sail, Danny." They heard the captain.

"I-yi, captain." One of the hands responded.

*Chick! Chickk! Chickkk!*

A golden orange flame shot up from the Zippo lighter which Uche held in his hand. Its illumination shined on his and his younger brother's faces. They looked down at an old mangled picture of their family. It was their mother, father, them and Boxy.

"Happier times." Uduka cracked a smile as he studied the photo.

"Yeah." Uche smirked. "Look at Boxy, always gotta be da bad ass." He pointed to the scowl of his late sibling.

They both laughed, wiping tears from the corners of their eyes, having shared stories about the deceased kin's exploits.

The remainder of the night they snacked on the food that they brought along and talked amongst each another, reminiscing about good times that their family shared. Suddenly, the brothers grew quiet as they were trapped within their thoughts, staring ahead at nothing. Uduka propped up his backpack and laid his head down against it, while Uche laid his head back against the wall. He swallowed as he closed his eyes and peeled them back open. They were glassy and twinkled with thoughts of revenge.

"We'll get'em brudda, every last goddamn one of dem." Uche swore. "I swear on it."

"We," Uduka began, snapping his brother's head in his direction, "swear on it." He held out his hand and his brother smacked his palm up against it, gripping it. He nodded.

They were going to America and they weren't returning until they had the head of their brother's killer.

Tranay Adams

# Chapter Six
## *A couple of nights later*

Tiaz and Threat sat in a van watching the block they'd been led to when they'd followed a black Chevy Suburban truck. The Suburban had been carrying what they'd deemed a very precious cargo, one Julian Carr. Their two million dollar meal ticket. Kantrell tailed the Suburban that had picked Juilan up from his home. They followed the bulletproof truck from the upper class area of Los Angeles to the slums of Compton. Once the Suburban was parked, a bald headed, refrigerator size Mexican man escorted Julian to what Tiaz and Threat believed was a trap house. They found out through Semaj, the cat that had put them onto the lick.

Smack, Julian's father, was a big time heroine dealer who was said to have a net worth of an estimated eleven million dollars. His son was a star basketball player at UCLA looking to be drafted. The boy was a serious pill head that liked to get faded and fuck like a porn star. The plan was to snatch him up and hold him down until they collected their two million dollar ransom.

Tiaz and Threat were all slouched down in the van, draped in black garments and wearing ski masks on their heads like beanies. Their hands were gloved and a taser gun was secured in the holsters on their chests.

"Fuck taking these niggaz so long? They been in there for like thirty minutes." Tiaz tapped his fingers on his knee impatiently.

Threat peered through the sideview mirror watching for police presence. "Why don't chu go knock on the door and tell'em to hurry up, so we can kidnap old boy?" he asked sarcastically. He looked to Tiaz and he was giving him the middle finger. He laughed and went back to staring into the sideview mirror.

"There they go." Threat nodded at the windshield. Julian and his bodyguard had just emerged from the trap house. "Hit cha girl, Crim."

"Alright." Tiaz called Kantrell through his Blu-Tooth headset. "Say, Lover, we're on."

"I got chu."

Now all they had to do was wait for their diversion. Kantrell's mission was to stick up the Food 4 Less off of Wilmington Avenue and give a couple of patrons some flesh wounds. This would draw the police to that location like flies to shit. The Sheriffs were as hot as firecrackers in Hub City, so The Boys would come pouring in droves. This was the diversion. Keep the law occupied until the thugs accomplished their task.

There was silence and then an eruption of gunshots from off in the distance. Not even a minute later, just as they expected, police car sirens filled the air and cruisers came zooming in from all directions.

"Man, let's get the fuck out of here." Julian high tailed it to the ebony beauty at the curb he was transported in.

"You read my mind." The fat head Mexican bodyguard replied, on his heels.

"It's time for some action, Jackson." Tiaz pulled the ski mask over his face, followed by Threat. The comrades hopped out of the van and moved in on their targets like a couple of ninja assassins. The bodyguard had just opened the rear passenger door for Juilan when Tiaz was about ten feet away. He accidently kicked over an empty 8 Ball can and the sound of it falling alerted the bodyguard.

The giant's head whipped around to him. He shoved Julian into the backseat of the Suburban and slammed the door closed. He drew his gun and extended it in Tiaz's direction. He was about to squeeze the trigger when the buff neck thug drew his taser gun and fired. The sharp ends of the cords stabbed into his chest and he yelled as the electricity shot through him. Yanking the cords from out of his pecks, he threw them to the ground, took aim at his assailant and opened fire. Tiaz ducked behind a car and drew his banger. He peeked out from behind the car and damn near got his face blown off. The bodyguard was advancing on him, busting his gun. Suddenly, the giant felt a sharp pain at the back of his skull. He touched it and came away with bloody fingertips. He swung his gun around and Threat slammed the butt of his banger into his nose, breaking it. The brute dropped his banger and cupped his gushing nose. Threat kicked him in the chest then tackled him, causing him to stagger backwards. He crashed to the sidewalk and the shorter man stood over him, pumping two into his heart.

*Boc! Boc!*

He looked up and saw his crime partner approaching the Suburban with a rag and a Zippo lighter. Tiaz knocked on the window of the truck.

"Get cho scary ass out of the truck, nigga!" he demanded of Julian. Straining his eyes, he peered through the tint and could see him shaking his head no. He held up the rag and the lighter. "All right, stay in there then. I'ma 'bout to blow this bitch up." He opened the gas tank door and stuffed the rag inside. Giving birth to a flame, he showed Julian before he lit the rag. He concealed the lighter then nudged Threat so they could clear the area before the truck exploded. They got about five feet before the rear passenger door of the Suburban flew open and their target hopped out. He tried to make a run for it, but Threat shot him with the taser-gun.

"Arghhh!"

His body went rigid and crashed to the sidewalk like a statue. Tiaz rushed over to the SUV and smacked the burning rag until he killed its flames. He then pulled it out and let it fall to the curb. He and Threat zip-cuffed the kid's wrists and ankles then gagged his mouth. They grabbed him under his arms and shoved him into the back of the van. Kantrell busted a U-turn and they left the block as quietly as they came.

\*\*\*

When Julian stirred awake, all he saw was darkness.

"Uhhh, hmmm." He thrashed around violently where he was perched, but the duct tape held him fast to the iron chair he was on. "Uhhh, Mmmmhuh." He attempted to scream, but the gag in his mouth muffled the noise. Suddenly, the black pillowcase was snatched from over his head. His eyes strained against the light illuminating from above. The bulb was only 40 watts, but seemed triple that since he'd been in the dark for hours. Fighting against the tense rays as he surveyed his surroundings, he saw three black blurs in front of him. He blinked his eyes and his vision slowly came into focus. He realized he was down in a basement along with three masked persons, one he assumed was a female from the long hair spilling out from underneath her mask. Terror in his eyes, Julian swallowed hard. He didn't know what he'd done to get himself in this situation, but he hoped he was able to see his way out of it alive.

The masked man facing Julian was the tallest of the trio. This nigga was huge, really fucking huge, almost the size of his bodyguard. The youngster could only imagine what he had planned for him if he didn't give him whatever he wanted. With this in mind, he trembled in his chair uncontrollably, scared for his life.

The tallest man was sitting backwards in an iron chair, smoking a smoldering blunt and watching him attentively. The fingers of his right hand were curled around the handle of a silver .357 magnum revolver. He blew a cloud of smoke into the boy's face, causing him to narrow his eyes and whip his head around. The taller masked man passed the blunt to his shorter accomplice that was leaned against a pillar. The shorter man took slow pulls and passed it to the mistress of the threesome. She was sitting on a sky blue milk crate with her legs crossed, clicking the safety on and off her weapon.

"All right, Junior, I'ma remove this gag, but if you scream I'ma shoot chu dead in your mouth. Do we understand each other?" Tiaz projected a cold stare with his menacing eyes, sending an icy chill up the young nigga'z spine that caused him to shiver like a December breeze. His voice was calm, but held an intense seriousness that let the star athlete know that he wasn't fucking around. The kid closed his eyes and swallowed his fear as best as he could, nodding yes. He then pulled the gag down from his mouth.

"What is all of this about?" Julian asked out of breath, chest twitching as his heart waged war inside of his chest. He was sweating bullets. The little nigga was scared as shit.

"Money." Tiaz took what was left of the L from Kantrell, sucking on the end of it. He lay back in his chair and blew out a roar of smoke in the college boy's direction, causing him to cough and narrow his eyes. "Your pops is handling a big pie and we want a slice. A very small slice. Two million dollars." He held up two fingers and used the other hand to tap his square, dumping ashes at his feet. "I think that's more than reasonable, considering what we could be asking for the apple of daddy's eye. The man is sitting on eleven mill, he probably uses the two we're asking for to maintain the upkeep of his property having Pedro trimming the hedges and picking the dog shit up from his lawn."

"What—what do you want me to do?" Julian asked with a shaky voice and bugged eyes, trembling.

"I'm gonna call daddy and I want chu to tell'em that you've been kidnapped." Tiaz told him. "You tell him we want two million dollars for your return and we aren't fucking around. If he refuses to un-ass that money, then I'm gonna kill you. It's as simple as two plus two."

"Okay, alright…" He hung his head and closed his eyes, taking a deep breath then exhaling. He threw his head back up and peeled his eyelids back open. "Two million dollars?" Tiaz nodded yes, blowing out more smoke. "Two mill, my dad can swing that. That's a little of nothing," he said to himself. Then he looked at the roughneck. "Okay, let's do it."

"Okay then." Tiaz picked up Julian's cell phone, removed the sim card, sat the cell on the seat of his chair, and used the butt of his revolver to smash it to pieces. Afterwards, he smacked the remains from the seat with the hand he used to hold his revolver. "GPS system. If pops put a bodyguard on you then I know he was keeping tabs on you." Placing the sim card into a burnout cell phone and turning it on, he scrolled through the contacts until he found the number listed as *Dad* and pressed *call*, listening as the phone rang. Once someone answered he placed the cell to the basketball star's ear.

"Hello, da—dad, it's—it's Julian." He spoke into the cell phone with a trembling voice. He only hoped that his old man could pull his ass out of the fire like he did so many other times before. *Lord, please*, he thought to himself. "I've been kidnapped. These men say they want two—two million dollars or they'll kill me. Oh my God, dad, you've gotta do something to get me out of here, these people aren't fucking around," he said in a panicked voice. He was so scared he could have wet his pants right then and there. "No games, dad, ones holding a big ass revolver to my face right now."

Tiaz took the cell phone from the kid's ear and held it to his own as he slowly walked around him. "What's up, Pops? It's Santa Claus, who the fuck do you think it is? It's the kidnapper, nigga. Now listen up, I want chu to bring two million dollars to...excuse me? Fuck me? Nah, nigga, fuck your son!" He pressed his banger into Julian's thigh and pulled the trigger. Julian's eyes bugged and he screamed like he caught his dick in a bear trap.

"Arhhhhh! Ahhhh! Ahhh!" He wailed uncontrollably, tears pouring down his cheeks. Tiaz disconnected the call and put the gag back into his mouth. The young boy's thigh was leaking profusely so he had Kantrell tighten a belt around it to slow the bleeding. He sat back down in the chair facing Julian, he held up five fingers and counted down, dropping a finger with each number he called out. The cell phone rang once he dropped the last finger and a shit eating grin spread across his face. He answered the call.

"Now, say you're sorry. Nah, not until you apologize. Apology accepted." Tiaz smiled. He went on to give Smack the address where they were to meet up and make the exchange. "Oh, and come alone, if I see anyone there besides you, I'ma send junior to that big basketball court in the sky. You've got two hours." He hung up the cell phone and slipped it into his pocket. He looked to Julian. "Daddy says he loves you." He kissed Julian on the side of his head then ruffled his hair. He then turned around to Threat and Kantrell, rubbing his hands together greedily. "All right, y'all, let's get this paper."

\*\*\*

Smack pulled into the closed Valero gas station parking lot in his champagne colored Cadillac ATS. He executed the engine and stepped out of the vehicle dressed in a brim, tailored Armani suit, which he wore under an overcoat, and black ostrich skin shoes. He closed the door and made his way to the back of the Cadillac. Afterwards, he popped the trunk and removed two big briefcases, one at a time. Sitting them both at his feet, he slammed the trunk closed and grabbed the briefcases by their handles, getting on his way. He walked to the end of the lot where he was to meet the kidnappers that had taken his son. Coming across the street, he spotted one of the most beautiful women he'd seen in quite some time. She was a cinnamon complexioned lovely that looked like she belonged somewhere sprawled on a sandy beach in a bikini taking pictures for the cover of Playboy magazine. Her eyes were hidden behind dark shades and she was casually smoking a cigarette while in motion. She was in a white blouse, which she wore a brown suede coat over, black leggings and brown leather high heeled boots. The boots echoed off the sidewalk with each step she took. She was moving toward Smack who was waiting at the end of the Valero gas station's lot. He was blowing into his cupped hands and rubbing them together, trying to keep warm. He was a bit nervous having to meet with the motha-fuckaz that snatched up his only son. For all he knew, they could flip the script and snatch his ass up, too, for an even bigger ransom.

The gorgeous woman flicked her cigarette aside and picked up the briefcases as she walked passed Smack. He looked on as she passed him, never uttering a word. He surveyed his surroundings and there wasn't a soul out that night, besides the two of them.

"Aye, where the hell is Junior?" he yelled out to the woman as she bent the corner at the end of the block. At that precise moment a van came to a screeching halt before him, startling him. Its side door slid open and Julian was shoved out. He collided with his father and they fell to the sidewalk. The van took off down the street, leaving them in each other's company.

Threat stared out of the back tinted window of the van at Smack and his son until they looked like dots from a distance. He then turned around and pulled off his ski mask, heading up front to Tiaz.

"All right, we gotta dump this bitch and burn her," Threat said of the stolen van.

"I already know. We're headed to do that now." He assured him.

Tiaz and Threat dumped the van, soaked it with gasoline and set it ablaze.

They hopped into a rented Dodge Charger and headed back out to Threat's house, where they chilled, swigging beers and waiting for Kantrell to arrive. Tiaz called and texted her, but she never answered. An hour passed and the two friends realized something was up. The duo hopped back into the Charger and headed over to her house. They knocked on the door first, but when they didn't get an answer, Tiaz used his keys to unlock the door.

The two men searched the house with their bangers leading the way. The house was quiet, really quiet. And as messy as Tiaz had remembered it, so he knew that old girl was gone, but still he couldn't help humoring himself with a search. Nonetheless, the pair advanced through the house, guns at the ready. Upon reaching Kantrell's bedroom, they searched her closet and dresser drawers. Both had been cleaned out. Tiaz's heart dropped, feeling like he'd been hoodwinked. A rage mounted in Threat and his face contorted into anger. He balled his fist and sent it slamming through the wall, creating a large hole. He then went around the bedroom tearing shit up, like a wild baboon released into civilization.

"This is all your fault!" Spittle flew from Threat's lips as he pointed his finger at Tiaz.

"My fault?" Tiaz pointed his thumb at his chest. He knew that Kantrell's ass was shadier than a Death Row contract, but he still fucked around with her. *Fucking snake, I thought I heard that bitch hiss a couple of times when she talked.* He shook his head. *Skeeza shitted on me like she shitted on Chevy, damn!*

"Yeah, nigga, your mothafucking fault!" Threat clarified. "You wanted to bring that bitch in on the lick. We could have gone at this shit on our own!"

Visibly angry, Tiaz shouted back. "Fuck you, Threat! I don't remember your ass objecting to bringing her on!"

"Fuck you!"

"Fuck you!"

"Nigga, fuck you." Threat tackled Tiaz into the wall, busting a hole in it. Tiaz punched him across the jaw and kicked him in the chest, sending him slamming into the nightstand, causing the flat screen to fall to the floor. Tiaz swung on Threat and he ducked him. The little nigga gave him two to the body and one to the head. He staggered to the right, but came back with a right cross that spilled Threat to the bed. He went to rush him and he kicked him in the chest. Tiaz went sailing back against the doorway and bumped the back of his head, leaving a smear of blood behind.

Before he could mount a defense, Threat was on him like a wolverine, raining combos on his face and head. For as small as Threat was, he was ferocious with his hands. Whether he had a gun, razor or his fists, he was a force to be reckoned with. He and Tiaz went at it like a couple of gladiators inside of an arena in Rome. Once the squabbling stopped, they were sprawled out on the floor, bleeding and breathing heavily.

"We gotta find this bitch, fam, before she gets away with our money." Tiaz told Threat as he lay on his back.

"She already has," Threat replied, getting upon his feet. "I'm pretty sure she's half way to wherever the fuck she's going by now." He held out his hand. Tiaz grabbed it and he pulled him upon his feet.

"My bad, Threat, I fucked up." Tiaz brought his hand down his face and exhaled. "I fucked up, man, big time." He admitted humbly.

"Don't worry about it." Threat patted him on the back. "Another score will fall in our lap again, and when it does we'll capitalize on it. Just the two of us." He motioned a finger between them.

"I swear to God if I ever cross paths with that bitch again, I'ma hold my boot to her chest and saw off her fucking head!" He exclaimed as Threat draped his arm over his shoulders and led him out of the bedroom.

### Meanwhile

Kantrell was sitting on the plastic covered couch at her next door neighbor's house. Her right hand rested in the pocket of her coat, clutching the handle of her Glock .23. The two big briefcases containing the two million dollars sat at her feet as she shook her crossed legs impatiently. Mr. Brown, an older yellow skinned man with a small graying afro peered out through the curtains. Once he'd seen Tiaz and Threat leave from in front of her house, he turned around to Kantrell.

"All right, they're gone now," he told her.

She rose from the couch and took a second glance through the curtains. Confirming that Tiaz and Threat were gone, she popped one of the briefcases open and stacked a few racks on the coffee-table for Mr. Brown's services. He thumbed through one of the stacks then tossed Kantrell the keys to his Buick Lesabre.

"Come on, help me put my stuff in the car." She told him as she picked up the two big briefcases holding the money. Mr. Brown grabbed her luggage and led her out the back door of the house and into the garage where his Buick Lesabre was stored. It was the perfect getaway car. It was teal green with a red driver's side door and a sunburned roof. No one would be expecting her to be driving it.

Bury Me A G 2

## Chapter Seven

Chevy stepped into the house after a long day's work. She'd spent twelve hours busting her hump and was due for a good night's rest. She had plans of collapsing on her bed and watching *The Walking Dead* marathon until she fell off. But then she was hit with a barrage of ideas for the remaining chapters of her book. She knew she'd have to put her thoughts out on paper quickly, otherwise she'd end up forgetting them.

Chevy couldn't get her jacket and utility belt off fast enough. She got her Apple laptop and its charger from her bedroom and brought it out to the living room. Having forgotten her ink pen and tablet, she headed back into her bedroom and retrieved them. She was about to step back into the living room when it dawned on her that she hadn't heard a peep out of Te'Qui since she'd been home. She knocked on his bedroom door and called out his name. When he didn't answer she pressed her ear against the door and listened in. Not hearing anything, she turned the door knob and walked inside. He was gone.

"Not again. Goddamn, Te'Qui."

Chevy called Helen and she said that the boys claimed that they were going to be at her house. She called Savon hoping that he'd have them, but he swore he hadn't talked to his nephew all that day. Afterwards, she hit Helen back up and told her that she didn't have to get out of bed, because she was going to hit the streets to look for the boys. Frustrated and pissed off, Chevy fired up her Caprice and hit the streets on a mission, looking for her baby boy. Turning down a dark residential block barely lit by the illumination of the streets lights, she saw a kid about Te'Qui's height in a hoodie posted on the corner. It appeared that he was standing out there slinging. She blinked her eyes twice, thinking that her mind was playing tricks on her. She couldn't believe what she was witnessing, her only child was posted up going hand-to-hand, curb serving.

Chevy wanted to roll upon Te'Qui and catch him in the act, but the gold Celebrity ahead was delaying her. The old raggedy car was slowly coasting up the block, holding up Chevy and about two cars behind her. She started to honk the horn, but she didn't want to draw his attention to her. When she got the notion to drive around the vehicle, it sped upon him. Her heart skipped a beat when she saw someone hang out the front passenger seat window with an MP-5. The gunman squeezed the trigger and flickers of light woke up the darkness as bullets spat from the machinegun. She screamed in horror as she watched bullets riddle her little boy's body. Crimson sprays misted the cold air and his form went crashing onto the sidewalk.

Chevy hopped out of her car and ran toward the body of her twitching son. "Oh God, please no, not my boy! Not my son!" The world had stopped spinning and everything had suddenly gone quiet. Save for her heart, she could hear it beating inside of her ears. *Thump! Thump! Thump! Thump!* Then there was her heavy breathing from her running. "Haa! Haa! Haa!" Tears pooled in her eyes as she advanced upon him, her nostrils flaring and mouth moving animatedly. She was running as fast and as hard as she could, but it felt like she was being held in place. Slowly, she brought her quivering hands toward her face.

\*\*\*

Te'Qui stood out on the corner with his head hidden beneath the hood of his sweater, rubbing his hands together trying to keep warm. It was as cold as Eskimo pussy outside and he could see his white smoke breath when he breathed. He had been posted up for all of three hours and had made four hundred dollars. He could see how one could become addicted to hustling. The money came fast and was plentiful. He kept a cautious look up and down the block. Though he had Baby Wicked posted up across the street from him keeping an eye out and holding him down with the .38 special, he still felt uneasy. He never knew when Maniac and Time Bomb were going to roll up on him. Whenever they did, he was sure that they would come rattling off automatic weapons. The thugs had warned him before about hustling on their corner, and had even told them if they ever saw them out there again that they'd come through busting heads.

Te'Qui knew that they were dead serious. At school he'd heard some of the kids whispering about the dirt they'd done. Nonetheless, it didn't matter. He knew the threats that the men posed, but he wanted a gold chain badly, badly enough to risk his life for one, as well as his friend's.

"Yo,' Wicked, let's switch up." He yelled across the street to his hustling partner. Wicked nodded and came across the street.

"It's cold as fuck out here," Wicked said, taking the tan rocks from his right hand and passing him the .38. The two boys exchanged jobs. Te'Qui took over the muscle and Wicked took over the slinging.

Wicked had just served a crack head, and was unwrinkling the bills he'd been paid with when he saw something moving out of the corner of his eye. He looked up and saw Maniac mad dogging him. For a moment, Maniac just stared at him, causing his stomach to twist into knots. He seemed to be speaking in slow motion and in a demonic voice, so Wicked caught everything he was saying. "I told you to stay the fuck off of our corner, cuz!" That's when the black MP-5 machinegun appeared in his hands out of thin air.

Wicked wanted to make a run for it, but his legs wouldn't cooperate with what his brain was telling them. The barrel of Maniac's MP-5 ignited and spat flames like a baby dragon, chewing the young nigga's body up something nasty. Lying on the corner, bloody and twitching, Wicked could hear the horrified screams of a woman, along with the screeching of tires as a car peeled off.

"Te'Qui?" Chevy looked down at the boy she thought was her son. Her tear stained face was one of confusion when she acknowledged that he wasn't him.

"Momma?" A voice came from her rear. She turned around and saw that it was her little boy, and a weight was lifted from off of her shoulders. She ran over to him and wrapped her arms around him. She hugged him so tight that he thought he heard his bones cracking up. "Oh, thank God you're alive. Were you hit?" She felt his body for gunshot wounds.

"No. I'm fine." Te'Qui looked to Wicked, his eyes were staring at nothing and his mouth was wide open. The Grim Reaper had claimed his soul and the only thing left was the vessel that his spirit inhabited. Te'Qui didn't know what to think or feel about seeing his friend murdered. He was without emotion, numb, like he'd taken a shot of Novocain.

Chevy heard police sirens in the distance. She did a 360 degree turn of the block as people were emerging from their homes. She knew that it was in her best interest to get the hell out of there. Te'Qui was more than likely dirty and she didn't want the police taking him when she'd just gotten him back. "Come on, we gotta get outta here." She grabbed Te'Qui's hand and ran toward her car.

\*\*\*

The morgue was as cold as a hooker's heart when Uche and Uduka entered. The staff working in the morgue led them over to a table at the far corner of the room. He gave them a look to see if they were ready for what they were about to see. The oldest of the brothers locked eyes with him and gave a nod. With the gesture made he threw the sheet back from their brother's body. Boxy's eyes were closed and his lips formed a tight line. He looked like he was asleep, but his bluish skin gave him away. That, and not to mention his limbs and head had been sewn back together. And now he resembled a black Frankenstein Monster.

"Is this him?" the worker asked.

"Yes. Dis is our brudda." Uduka answered, as his palm caressed Boxy's cold forehead. His eyes became glassy and the pain of his loss expanded in his chest. He squeezed his eyelids closed and tears shot down his dark cheeks. Inside of his head, he saw Boxy strapped down to a table while some sick bastard hacked off different body parts. He saw his brother's eyes stretched wide open bleeding with pain as he screamed at the top of his lungs, showcasing all of his cavities. He could only imagine the excruciation his sibling must have felt before he met with his death.

"I'll give you two a minute." Seeing the pain in the youngest Eme brother's face, the worker sympathetically opted to leave the room.

"Look wat has been done ta our brudda, Uche." Uduka spoke with teary eyes. "Muddafuckaz!" He slammed his fist down against the metal slab, causing it to ring and echo throughout the room. "Dey tortured him, man, dey fucking tortured him! Den dey cut 'em up like he was fuckin'...fuckin' sushi!" He threw up a hand.

Uche looked down at Boxy while gripping his younger sibling's shoulder.

"His death will not go unpunished, I swear on our father's honor. Everyone involved shall answer fa dis." He spoke with his eyes still on his brother's cadaver.

"Indeed dey will." Uduka wiped his dripping eyes with the back of his fist. While the younger brother responded to their relative's death with grieving and tears, the oldest responded with a deeper resolve to avenge their brother's death. Their hurt, their pain, their turmoil, those responsible would feel all of this, right before they met with a gruesome death.

"Look at me." Uche ordered. His brother turned around. They locked eyes as he gripped his shoulders. "We show no mercy to deez people dat are involved. Family, friends, whoeva we godda go through to get to 'em, gets it. Agreed?" Uduka nodded. "Fa Boxy." He extended his opened hand.

"Fa Boxy." He smacked hands with his loved one, pulling him in and embracing.

Uche listened as his kin sobbed loud and hard into the breast of his suit. His hand swept up and down his back as he tried to soothe his pain. As the youngest, Uduka was definitely the most sensitive out of the Eme Brothers. While the others hid their emotions or rarely showed them, he didn't have any problems with displaying his. "Shed ya tears, shed them all, for da days to come we shall shed blood."

The Eme brothers made the arrangements to send their brother back home. With this done, they moved to carry out their mission: eradicating their enemies. They realized when they touched down in America within the depths of their souls that their lives would never be the same after the horrors they were about to commit. There wasn't any doubts in their minds that they would get an all expenses paid, first class ticket to hell, once they were done and that was quite alright with them, just as long as their brother got to rest in peace.

\*\*\*

"Where to?" The Gypsy cab driver looked over his shoulder.

"Motel. A nice one, please," Uduka answered.

"Neva mind ma brudda," Uche spoke up, holding up a hand. "Take us to the nearest motel." Feeling Uduka's eyes on him, he looked into his direction to find his inquisitive eyes. "We're not heah on a vacation, we're heah on business." His eyes darted to the driver then back to his little brother, speaking in a hushed tone. "We're heah ta find our brudda's keela. Don't get sidetracked by anytin' else. Keep ya mind." He jabbed his finger at his temple. "On da mission at hand, ya undastand me?" Uduka closed his eyes and nodded his head. Peering back up at his brother, he knew that he was right. They didn't want to get too relaxed while in the states. They could get caught slipping and end up in a bad way, if they didn't remain on point.

Hearing commotion coming from outside, the brothers peered out of the window. They saw two men arguing over the point in a dice game.

"Nigga, yo' point was ten!" A cat rocking cornrows and a white T-shirt shouted.

"Man, my point was foe!" A baldheaded dude came from under his hoodie with a knife.

When homie sporting the cornrows pulled a gun from his waistline and pointed it at him, all of the hoe ran up from out of him. He dropped his knife and his hands shot up in the air as he took a step back. The rest of the gamblers scrambled away, abandoning their money and alcoholic beverages.

*Bow! Bow! Bow!* Cornrows walked upon his kill and picked up his money, kicking his lifeless body.

"Like I said mothafucka, your point was ten." He told the corpse, spitting on his face. He then looked up and locked eyes with Uche and Uduka. He tucked his banger on his waistline and walked away casually from the scene. The Eme brothers settled down in their seats and exchanged perturbed glances.

### *Seven minutes later*

Uche paid the cab driver and secured a room at the Western Inn. Their minds were so preoccupied with finding their brother's killers that they didn't pay any attention to their surroundings. It was like they were in a trance and only one thing mattered to them, vengeance. Walking in, Uche dropped his bag by the table and chair and so did Uduka.

When he plopped down on the bed and slipped off his shoes, his brother went on to talk.

"Uche, I think we should get ourselves some guns if we're gon' look for Boxy's keelas," Uduka began. "There's no way we can..."

"No! No, no, no." He shook his head as he slipped his wife beater over it.

"Did you not see what happened out there tonight? Dat mon was killed, like dat." He snapped his fingers.

"I don't care, guns are fa' cowards," he claimed. "It tis wit deez." He held up his fists. "Or dis." He picked up his spear. "Dat truly exerts ya strength as a mon."

"True." Uduka nodded. "But we're in America now, my brudda. And tis da way of da gun dat deez people gravel ta, not da spear. If we go out dere now wit only our bare fists and deez weapons, den we will be cut down before we avenge our brudda."

*Fuckin' Uche neva listens to me, stubborn bastard! It's always his way or dee highway. He has to see things the way that I see dem or we're gon' get keeled before we've found Boxy's keelas.*

Uche sighed and hung his head. He massaged his chin as he thought on it. Looking up at his little brother, he said, "Okay. But where are we gonna get deez guns?"

"Hmmm," Uduka massaged his chin as he gave it some thought. He snapped his fingers once he came to the conclusion. "The hood."

\*\*\*

Chevy sat on the couch smoking a cigarette in deep thought. She'd put Te'Qui through an intense interrogation when they made it back home. Asking where did he get the drugs from? When did he start hustling? How long he'd been hustling? And why he was slinging? The juvenile answered every question except where he'd gotten the drugs from. She slapped him upside the head and fired on him a couple of times, before sending him off to his bedroom.

Next, she got with Faison and gave him the rundown about what happened that night. He was relieved that his son was okay and told her he'd be by there as soon as he handled some very important business.

Chevy disconnected the call and started to dial up Baby Wicked's Aunt Helen. She was in the middle of punching the numbers when she heard a shrill from the outside. Still holding the telephone, she darted to the window and peered through the curtains.

"Oh my God, not him, not my Brice!" She saw Helen crying in the arms of a detective as he tried to comfort her.

Chevy hung up the phone and stepped away from the window, shaking her head. She decided to wait until tomorrow to tell her about what had happened. Helen was dealing with great grief now and she didn't want to disturb her.

Chevy had an idea where Te'Qui had gotten the narcotics from, but she hoped that she was wrong. She had to find out to be sure though. Figuring that there was no place to get her information from than the source, she placed a call to Tiaz. When he didn't pick up, she blew up his cell phone until he answered. She told him that she had a situation and that she needed him to come over right away. He told her that he'd be over in thirty minutes and that was an hour ago.

Chevy was growing impatient by the minute. Every so often she'd glance at the digital clock on her cell phone and take a peek through the curtains to see if Tiaz had pulled up yet. In that two hour span she'd damn near went through a fresh pack of Newports. Coming from the curtains after taking a quick peek, she picked up her carton of squares from the coffee table. She withdrew one from the wrinkled pack with her lips and started to light it when she heard someone at the door. She slipped the cigarette back into the pack and tossed it beside the ashtray on the coffee table.

Tiaz came through the door and locked it behind him. He wore a worried expression on his face. Chevy had called him in hysterics demanding that he come over right away. He had no idea what she'd wanted, or what had transpired in his absence. He figured some of Majestic's people had found where he used to lay his head and were holding Chevy and Te'Qui hostage, that's why he already had his pistol brandished when he came through the door.

"You, alright?" Tiaz asked, looking around the house.

"I'm fine."

"What's wrong with you?" He inquired of the expression of anger on her face.

"Take a good goddamn guess." She frowned and snaked her neck, folding her arms to her chest, waiting for his response.

"Look, are you gon' tell me what's up or not?" Tiaz asked, annoyed, tucking his banger into his waistline and then opening the refrigerator. He removed a bottle of Heineken and twisted off the cap.

"You got my kid out on the streets pushing drugs for you?" Chevy blurted with attitude, eyebrows lowered to form a scowl.

She was ready to explode. She trusted, loved, supported and sheltered this nigga, and he fucked her best friend. And now she was pretty goddamn sure that he had her son hustling crack out in the streets.

"What?" His forehead wrinkled. His heart rate sped up. He was nervous, being that these were serious allegations and he was still on parole. One phone call to The Boys and he was back on the bus, shackled, getting transported back to prison.

"You heard what I said."

"Fuck I look like having your boy pushing dope for me?" He took a swig of the beer.

"So, you don't have Te'Qui and his friend out there pumping for you?"

"No."

"You a goddamn lie, I found this in the garage." She held up half a brick of cocaine. "I was wondering what you were always doing in the garage, and look what I found."

"That's not mine." He lied with a straight face.

"Why are you lying, man? If there are two things I can't stand it's a liar and a cheater. You know Te'Qui was almost *murdered* tonight on that corner? He got lucky, but his friend..." She choked up as an image of Baby Wicked being gunned down swept through her mind. "They shot'em down like a dog. I could have sworn I heard that little boy crying out for his momma." Her eyes became glassy.

"Well, that ain't my fault, sweetheart. You need to holler at the cat that put the lil' niggaz on the corner. Don't worry, you find his sorry ass and me and this Beretta of mine will make sure he never puts another package of dope in another shorty's hands again."

The skin on Chevy's forehead bunched together and her eyes narrowed. She coiled her neck as she looked at Tiaz like he was a complete stranger. She couldn't believe that this was the same man that had written her those sweet letters and swept her off of her feet. This nigga standing before her was cold, calculating, and didn't give two shits about her or her son. He'd almost put their lives, safety and freedom at stake and refused to take responsibility for what he'd done.

"Nigga, who the fuck are you?" Her brows furrowed.

"You know who I am," he replied, taking the beer from his lips.

"You know what, Tiaz? I bet chu don't even really have a job, do you? You and Threat be out there in the streets knocking niggaz over, huh?" Tiaz shrugged and took a swig of his beer. "Hmmph." She shook her head. "You know what? You and I are officially through, your ass is fired!" Chevy told him coldheartedly.

"What chu saying?" He sat his beer down on the table.

"Okay, let me break it down for you in laymans terms. I'm dumping you. Get the fuck outta my house!" She pointed to the door.

"Fuck you think you're talking to?" He looked at her like she'd lost her mind talking to him like that.

Chevy put her hands on her hips. "You."

Tiaz was heated. He'd spent the majority of his life in institutions. He'd been housed with some of the state's most unsavory characters. Hard body niggas that most cats would cross the street to get away from. He hadn't let any of them run a foul at him, so he sure as hell wasn't about to let some broad come at him as if he were a lesser man. He was already tight about Kantrell stiffing him for two million dollars. Now, he had Chevy in his face totally disrespecting him. Enough was enough. He had finally reached his breaking point.

Tiaz stared straight ahead. Something within his mind snapped like a twig. His right eye twitched and lips moved animatedly. He made weird sounds as his entire head vibrated. He was burning up, set a blaze, on fire, scorching. "Grrrr!" He roared, hauling off and cracking Chevy dead in her eye, causing her to spin around and hit the floor. She wore a shocked expression while down on her hands and knees. She couldn't believe that he had punched her. No man had ever put their hands on her.

"Bitch, who in the fuck you think you talking to like that?" He stalked Chevy from behind as she crawled on the floor. She made to pull herself up by grabbing a hold of the kitchen sink and he kicked her in the side. She hit the floor and bumped the side of her head. He went to kicking and punching her like she'd stolen something. Then he whipped out his gun and *Click! Clacked!* one in its head, extending it toward the back of Chevy's dome. "That's yo' ass, hoe!" His finger applied pressure to the trigger.

"Argggghhh! Fuck!" Tiaz dropped his head bussa and grabbed his arm after feeling a sharp pain in it. He touched it and came away with blood. He looked up and saw Te'Qui holding a smoking Taurus .9mm. His face was twisted in a mask of anger as he bit down on his bottom lip, daring the thug to make another move.

"Get the fuck away from my momma." The little nigga barked.

"Lil' nigga, you must have lost your mind, pulling that strap out on me!" Tiaz gritted his teeth. "I'ma take that gun, stick it up your ass, and pull the trigger until I hear it click!" He moved to do harm to Te'Qui and the vase behind him exploded, startling him.

"The next one going in your dome, fool," Te'Qui swore.

"No, baby, don't do it." Chevy pleaded to her son as she slowly got to her feet, wincing and holding her side.

"Fuck this nigga!" Te'Qui fumed, staring Tiaz down, face twitching with anger.

"I respect your G, lil' homie. Salute." Tiaz saluted him. "But chu better kill me, 'cause if I leave here with my life, I will return to collect yours. Here, let me help you out." He dabbed his finger in the bleeding hole in his arm and rubbed the blood at the center of his forehead, creating a bull's eye. "There's your target, put one right there." He leaned his forehead forth so he could get a clean shot at him.

"No, baby, don't listen to him." Chevy pleaded with her son.

For a time Te'Qui stood there staring into the thug's eyes and debating on whether he should kill him or not. Hearing his mother in his ear begging him not to oblige Tiaz, he lowered his gun at his side and said, "Get out of our house."

"Damn, and here I thought some of me had rubbed off on you." Tiaz shook his head in disappointment as he headed for the front door.

Chevy took her Taurus .9mm away from Te'Qui and pulled him close for an embrace. She held him tight as tears slid down her cheeks. The youngster peered over his mother's shoulder, staring off at nothing. He was terribly conflicted. One of the men he looked up to turned out to be a real scum bag. He broke his mother's heart and beat on her. He wanted to murder that ass so badly, but she stopped him. On top of that he saw his best friend get murdered in cold blood that night.

Te'Qui had a smorgeshbord of emotions inside of him that he didn't know how to address. He knew that he felt sad and wanted to cry, but for some reason his eyes wouldn't permit it. Although the tears wouldn't fall on the outside, he knew that they were falling on the inside.

He closed his eyes and lay his head up against his mother's, holding her firmly in his arms and wishing that night was just a bad dream.

# Chapter Eight
## *A couple of days later*

*Buzzzzz!*

The gate of the prison alerted before sliding back, granting another convict his freedom. Wicked walked out of captivity, narrowing his eyelids and grimacing as he stared up into the sky. The sun was shining its brightest that day and he thought it was the most beautiful sight in the world. It was funny to him how the smallest things in life became that much more important when they were denied. Things like coming and going as he pleased, eating what he wanted day to day, showering when he wanted, a cozy bed, fresh air, pussy. The most common things in life became more precious than gold when someone was locked up. And he didn't realize how much they meant to him until they were taken away.

Wicked slipped on a pair of black sunglasses and took a deep breath, inhaling the stale air. Although it was tainted, it tasted of something he'd been longing for the past fifteen months, freedom. A slight smirk curled the corner of his lips as he took a good look at his surroundings, searching for his ride. He stole a glance at his watch and looked up just in time to see a BMW tearing up the road, leaving a line of dust in its wake. He hoisted his sack of goods over his shoulder and started for the car. He got about five feet before the sexy red machine came pulling to a stop in front of him.

The driver side door opened and red pumps stepped out one at a time. A hefty body in a red dress came into view, gripping the edge of the doorway with red tipped finger nails. The face Wicked took in was the one that belonged to his Aunt Helen. She wore a big hat and designer shades that covered most of her face. Her cheeks were slicked wet so it was apparent that she'd been crying. She removed the shades and wiped her eyes with a balled up tissue. This made Wicked's heart quicken and his face ball up.

"Aunt Helen, what's wrong?" He dropped his sack of goods and approached his Aunt. He was five feet away from her when she threw herself into him, wrapping her arms around him. She sobbed loud and hard into the chest of his shirt. He kept asking her what was wrong, but she wouldn't say anything. She just kept right on crying, like there was no tomorrow. He tightened his embrace and swept his hand up and down her back, whispering something into her ear to comfort her.

### *Three hours later*
Wicked paced the living room floor, chain smoking and occasionally glancing over at his Aunt Helen. Her face was sprawled with dried white streams and she was under a blanket sound asleep. As soon as they left the prison, they shot straight over to Denny's where they ate Grand Slams and discussed what had happened to Baby Wicked. She'd been crying and reminiscing about his younger brother for the greater part of the evening. On the way home she insisted on him buying her a six pack of beer and a little something to burn down.

She was good and shit faced by the time they made it to the house. She polished off the last two beers and went on an epic rant about how God was coming back and how they all were going to be made to pay for their sins. Afterwards she crashed on the couch and cried until sleep took her.

Wicked mashed out his cigarette and poured a drink. Entering his bedroom, he grabbed the portrait of him and his brother and threw himself on the bed. He stared at the portrait as he took slow, casual sips of the alcohol. It felt good to be back home, lying in a nice, comfortable bed, being able to have a decent meal and partake in the spoils of freedom. As badly as he wanted to, he couldn't enjoy these luxuries just yet. Nah, he had a very serious matter that called for his attention. It had to be taken care of ASAP. That was finding the dick suckers that stole his brother's life and making them pay for putting their hands on his family.

Wicked and Baby Wicked were the only two boys of Caroline and Rubert Michaels. One night, their mother, while on her way home from the supermarket had gotten raped. The boys' father took it upon himself to go looking for the bastards that had violated his lady. There were four of them. He lined them up on the alley down on their knees. He went down the row, placing his revolver to the back of their heads, and pulling the trigger, killing them execution style. That night, he'd gotten way, but eventually the police caught up with him. He was sentenced to death. Not willing to let her sons' father face death by lethal injection, Caroline tried to spring her husband from the belly of the Beast.

Before the couple could make it to the outside, they were cut down by rifles. They died side by side, holding each another's hands. The tragedy left their children orphans until the Robert's Aunt Helen took them in.

Wicked had been brainwashed by his big homie, Krazy, before him. His OG had him doing despicable acts that would make even the devil cringe. The same evil he introduced Wicked to, was the same he poisoned his little brother with. Some could say that the oldest of the Michaels boys was the spawn of Satan. He'd done some Michael Myers type of shit. Hell, he'd earned his name carving an enemies' tongue out of his mouth while he dangled from a tree in a park. Look up psychopath in the dictionary and there would be a picture of his deranged ass.

Wicked couldn't help but to think back to how he may have poisoned his brother's brain with the same bullshit he was taught. Instead of steering him away from gangbanging, he turned the young nigga on to it. The crazy thing was that he was actually proud about how he'd corrupted the adolescent. To him, grooming little niggaz to be exactly like him gave him a sense of accomplishment, like a medal of honor or some shit. This was how twisted his way of thinking was.

*Wicked pushed the G-ride, occasionally looking over to the front passenger seat at Baby Wicked. Then the eleven year old nigga was drunk and high. It was his first time getting shit faced, so needless to say the effects of the alcohol and weed hit him quite hard. Wicked had taken the liberty of getting his little brother faded to ease his nerves for the night's mission. The homies had seen what he could do with his hands, so he was already in, but Wicked wanted to see if he had it in him to kill something. Since the boy was going to be wearing his name, he had to be with the shit. He had to be a killer just like his brethren.*

*Baby Wicked's eyes were hooded and bloodshot. He rode shotgun, taking draws from the roach end of the blunt pinched between his fingers, polluting the interior with funky white smoke. Once he was finished, he flicked what was left of it out of the window and expelled the last of the smoke from his nose. He was relaxed and ready to put in work now.*

*"Alright, there them niggaz go." Wicked peeped a gathering of people at a barbeque that were none the wiser to death looming over their heads like a dark cloud. There were a mixture of kids, adults and Crips out there, but he didn't give a fuck. The enemy or anybody affiliated with them was just as good, just as dead.*

*"Them?" Baby Wicked's forehead creased. "But there's kids out there, too."*

*"And?" Wicked raised an eyebrow. "Lil' crabs grow up to be big crabs." Click! Clack! He chambered a hollow tip bullet into the compact black handgun. "Here you go." He passed the head bussa to the youngster. He looked from the gun in his gloved hand to his big brother. An evil grin curled his lips, feeling the power surge through his body having the Death Dealer in his hands. He felt like a God now. He had the ability to take life. It was incredible.*

*Wicked executed the headlights and brought the old school to a crawl, it was moving slow like its passengers were looking for a parking space.*

*"Who do you want me to get?" Baby Wicked threw the hood from off of his head.*

*Wicked shrugged and smiled, showcasing a top row of gold shiny teeth which spelled out his name WICKED. "Shieettt, bullets ain't got no name. Old niggaz, young niggaz, blind, cripple or crazy, take yo' pick. It don't matter. Anybody can get it."*

*"Sho' you right."*

*Baby Wicked emerged from out of the front passenger window extending the handgun, both hands wrapped around it.*

*When the people at the cookout spotted him, some froze while others fled, screaming for their lives.*

*"He's gotta gun!" One shouted.*

*"Oh shit!" Another panicked.*

*"Run!"*

*Poc! Poc! Poc!*

Wicked shook the hard truth from his head, his brother's demise wasn't his fault. Nah, the way he saw it, the young nigga was old enough to make his own decisions. Baby Wicked was thirteen years old, and in the hood that was considered a grown ass man. That made him responsible for his own actions and the choices he made. Wicked wasn't about to carry the burden of his sibling's murder on his shoulders. He had enough shit he was dealing with internally. His death was on the fools that murdered him and he was going to see to it that everyone involved met a bloody death.

Wicked sat the portrait down on the dresser and leaned his head back against the pillow. He took a sip and rested the glass on his chest twisting it around, as he stared up at the ceiling.

*Nah, that shit ain't on me. And whoever it is betta hope I don't find 'em, on Blood gang,* he thought closing his eyes and thinking about what he was going to do to the cat that had murked his brother. An evil smile etched across his face as he saw himself pumping round after round into his face.

Wicked knew that the cycle of violence would most likely continue. Even if he did track the niggaz down that popped his kid brother, who was to say that their people wouldn't ride back on him? They'd murder him and his homies would get them. It would keeping going and going, forever and ever. He didn't give a mad ass fuck though. He wouldn't stop until them fools that did his loved one bad got their issue.

### The next day

Te'Qui looked up into the sky as a flock of birds soared above. The day was bright and beautiful, the complete opposite of how he felt inside, dark and ugly. He was in the hour that he was to bury his best friend. All he felt was anger and sorrow. At times he thought he was going to cry. There was a stinging in his eyes, but the tears wouldn't come. It wasn't that he was forcing them back. It was that they refused to manifest. He didn't know it, but this was the beginning stages of his heart hardening. Te'Qui felt a hand on his shoulder. He looked over it and found his mother beside him. She was wearing a big hat with a flower on the side of it and oversized designer shades. Chevy wasn't particularly fond of the shades, they clashed with the floral dress that she had on. But they did an excellent job of hiding the black eye Tiaz had given her.

"Come on, baby, let's go inside." Chevy told Te'Qui, as she grasped his hand, wincing.

Te'Qui's forehead wrinkled with worry seeing his mother in pain. "You all right, ma?" he questioned with concern.

"Uh huh." She mustered a half hearted smile, putting up a front for her little man. She was still quite sore from the beating Tiaz had handed down, but she'd get better in time.

Together, Chevy and Te'Qui made their way up the stone steps and then through the doors of the church. As soon as they crossed the threshold they heard the wails and sobs of a woman sitting somewhere up front. Te'Qui looked at the faces of the many men and women that filled up the pews of the holy sanctuary. Some were wet with tears, some were crying, while others were solemn.

Te'Qui looked over his shoulder and saw a cluster of Bloods standing up in the back. The men were eye sores with their red attire. Some wore an article of red clothing, while others were in red from head to toe. Te'Qui noticed a very familiar face amongst them. He was a 5'10, African American man with a youthful, chubby face and a brown skin tone. He had black rings under his eyes and sported his hair in six neat cornrows, tied off at the back by a red rubber band. He was in a red button down shirt and slacks. His hands were folded at his waist and he was staring straight ahead. His face was void of any expression. The man was Baby Wicked's older brother, Big Wicked.

Big Wicked was a man with an extensive rap sheet that ranged with everything from rape to murder. He'd earned his name committing some of the most despicable acts one could imagine. He wore his deeds like a badge of honor and didn't have any qualms about discussing them.

Wicked saw Te'Qui and gave him a half hearted grin and a nod. Te'Qui returned the gesture and continued up front with his mother. They sat across from the woman who was doing all of the wailing and sobbing. Te'Qui took a peek from where he sat beside his mother and saw that the woman was Baby Wicked's aunty, Helen. He felt terrible seeing her crying and carrying on. She'd raised Baby Wicked and his brother after their parents had been murdered. Aunty Helen was an all right woman and a decent enough caretaker. She didn't have a lot, but she did alright for herself. Most of her money came from the older gentleman that she entertained. With that money and what she got from her social security check at the end of every month, she was able to pay for her rent, the necessities and get herself a few things. All of the extras Baby Wicked got were from his brother's hustling or him breaking bad out on the streets. Te'Qui sat back in his seat, laying his head against his mother's shoulder. Chevy locked her fingers between her son's fingers and kissed him on the top of his head. Together they watched the minister step to the podium and begin the sermon.

Once Baby Wicked's coffin was in the ground, the mourners went off on their own heading for their cars. Te'Qui and Chevy were walking towards their car when he spotted Savon talking to Wicked.

"Momma, I wanna say goodbye to Wicked before we leave." Te'Qui told his mother.

"Alright, I'll be in the car." She told him before walking off toward the car.

"Wicked, can I talk to you for a minute?" Te'Qui interrupted Savon and Wicked's conversation.

"Sure."

"Where's your momma, nephew?" Savon asked.

"She went back to the car," Te'Qui answered.

"Alright," Savon patted him on the shoulder as he moved past him.

"What's up with chu, Y.G.?" Wicked slapped hands with Te'Qui once Savon had gone.

"Ain't shit, kinda fucked up behind your brotha, though," he admitted, looking away to hide the hurt in his eyes.

"Me, too, that was my lil' nigga. My mothafucking heartbeat, nah what I'm saying?" He patted his fist over his heart. "But best believe I'm gon' find the niggaz that peeled my lil' bro and let these two nines of mine share my grievances. You ain't gotta worry about nothing, lil' homie, your friends death will be avenged." He assured him.

"I know who killed him," Te'Qui confessed.

Wicked leaned closer to him, putting his hand on his shoulder and asking, "Who?"

"I'll tell you, but first you gotta promise to let me roll on'em with you and let me get my officials," Te'Qui said.

"Alright." he nodded.

"Nah, put that on your brotha, that you gone let me ride with chu."

Wicked blew hard and massaged the bridge of his nose. "Alright, that's on baby bro that if you tell me who his killer is that I'll let chu roll with me."

"Okay." Te'Qui began. "There were two of them, Maniac and Time Bomb."

"How do you know this?"

"Me and Baby Wicked were serving in their hood and they rolled up and popped him."

Wicked shook his head. It was a dumb move for his brother and his friend to be hustling in a hood that wasn't their own. Anything went on foreign soil. The enemy could give them a pass or he could make them pay the price for trespassing. Wicked stood erect, looking down at Te'Qui. "Okay, Blood, I'ma come by your house when it's time to get with these niggaz. You just be ready."

"I stay ready so I ain't gotta get ready." Te'Qui slapped hands with him and made his way toward his mother's car. As he neared the car he could see Savon shouting something at his mother.

\*\*\*

"Damn, girl, slow down." Savon said jogging up behind Chevy. She stopped and turned around.

"What's up, Savon?" she asked as she searched her purse for her car keys.

"You," he answered. "You've been avoiding me the past few days. Hell, you even ducking me at the funeral. What's going on?"

"Life, baby brother. That and tryna help Te'Qui cope with losing his best friend," she admitted. What she wasn't telling him was that Tiaz had given Te'Qui and Baby Wicked drugs to sell, and that he'd given her a black eye. "He acts like he isn't fazed, but I can see it in his eyes that he's hurting."

"Yeah, I know how it can be. I've lost plenty of homies." When she brought her head up from searching her purse, the sunlight hit her face at an angle that exposed her black eye to Savon. "What happened to your face?"

"What're you talking about?" Chevy played dumb.

"Your eye," Savon said. He went to reach for her shades. She tried to grab his wrist, but she wasn't fast enough. Savon removed the shades from her eyes and exposed her black, swollen eye. "Who punched you in your eye?"

"Nobody, I fell."

"It was Faison, wasn't it?"

"No!"

"Then who?" When Chevy looked away, Savon knew that it was Tiaz that had done the damage. "That mothafucka is dead! You hear me? Nigga, put his hands on mine, I'ma chop off whatever hand he raised to you!"

"Savon, it's not that serious! Let it go! It's over between us, I'm moving on." Chevy assured him. She didn't want him to go off and kill Tiaz, because if he were to get caught that would be his third strike. The last thing she wanted to do was go on living knowing that she was responsible for her brother being incarcerated for the rest of his life.

Chevy tried to grab her brother's arm as he stormed off, but he yanked away. She pleaded for him not to kill Tiaz as he hopped into his Camero and sped off.

Te'Qui had come walking up just as his uncle sped off. He approached his mother. "He knows, huh?"

Chevy nodded wearing a pitiful look on her face. "He saw my eye."

He embraced his mother, hugging her tight and rubbing her back as she cried.

***

Tiaz stepped out of the liquor store with his thick fingers wrapped around a 40 oz bottle of Olde English. He gave the block a quick scan before taking the malt liquor to the head, guzzling it. He brought the bottle down from his lips and used the back of his hand to wipe his mouth. He bopped his way down the sidewalk heading towards his whip. A man in a hood was approaching him with his hands concealed in the pockets of his hoodie. Tiaz's heart thumped in his chest. His street instincts kicked in and his hand moved for the banger on his waistline. He was about to pull out and riddle the hooded man with hollow points when he pulled off his hood and spoke.

"Aye, boss, you gotta light?" The man held up a cigarette.

Tiaz nodded. He went to retrieve the Zippo lighter from the breast pocket of his tan Dickie shirt. He'd just pulled it when the dim streetlight bounced off of something in the man's hand, causing it to gleam. He saw that the man was drawing a chrome .44 Magnum. His eyes bugged then they formed a scowl, he dropped his lighter and went to brandish his banger, but he was way too slow on the draw. The butt of the .44 slammed into the side of his skull, sending him stumbling back and slumping against the fence. Sitting up on the ground, he saw stars and half moons before his eyes. With all of the people he'd shitted on in his lifetime a million names, faces and situations raced through his brain. This ass whopping could have been for a number of reasons. He was sure of one thing though, if murder were on the mind of these men, he wouldn't live long enough to find out.

Tiaz felt a hand pull the banger free from his waistline and then he heard a whistle. The sharp noise brought forth two henchman dressed in all black from the shadows. He attempted to get upon his feet and the man gripping the .44 kicked him in the ribs. The buff neck thug fell on his back. He tried to get up again and feet and fists rained down upon his hide. He grimaced and rolled around on the ground.

Savon had been sitting on the hood of his Camero watching the whole scenario, while smoking a cigarette. Only when he yelled out *"That's enough"* did the assault on Tiaz cease. He blew smoke into the air and let his square drop to the ground. Once he mashed the square out under the heel of his sneaker, he pulled the black snub nose revolver from the small of his back. In no rush, he approached the thug in a slow and calm stride, as if he was taking a stroll in the park.

"Lift him up."

He told his homeboys as he brought his foot upon the curb. The homies grabbed Tiaz under his arms and held him up. His head was hung so Savon could only see the top of it. Pulling up the legs of his jeans, he stooped down and grasped his bottom jaw, clutching the lower half of his face so tight that he groaned in pain. Savon lifted his head so that he'd be staring him in the eyes. Right after he stuck his pistol in between his busted lips, causing him to gag a little.

"Listen and listen good, cock sucka." Savon's face hardened and his nostrils flared. "If I ever hear about you coming near my sister or my nephew again, I swear on everything that I love, I'ma blow your mothafucka brains out, you hear?" He cracked Tiaz across the head with his gun and he fell over on his side. He then stomped him twice and kicked him in the stomach, knocking the wind out of him. Tiaz lay on the ground holding his stomach and wincing in pain.

*Bitch ass nigga,* Tiaz thought to himself, *outta all of the gangstas, killerz, and shotcallers I've locked ass with, I almost got taken out by this tall, pretty mothafucka. Ain't this about a bitch? That's alright. You should have finished me off when you had the chance, homeboy, 'cause payback is a bitch.*

Savon tucked his gun into the front of his pants and waved his crew on. "Let's get outta here." He walked off with them bringing up the rear.

***

"Do you know who did it?" Threat asked from the other side of the phone.

"Yeah, I know exactly who did it." Tiaz spoke into his cell phone, heatedly. He was as hot as fish grease about having his ass handed to him by Savon and his goons. When he'd taken inventory of his injuries in the hospital's rest room, he had a black eye, busted lips and stitches in his forehead and one of his fingers was in a cast.

Tiaz shuffled through the automatic doors of County General hospital with a brown paper bag of painkiller medication.

"Who? Tell me who it is and I'ma light a spark in his dome. I'm my brotha's keeper." Threat swore.

"Chevy's lil' brotha, Savon, but don't worry I'ma take care of that Chico Debarge looking mothafucka. I got something for his punk ass."

"You want me to come get chu?"

"Nah, I'ma catch a cab home, I'll rap with chu later, Crimey, deuces." He hung up his cell phone and put it in his pocket. He then waved down a cab. He hopped into the backseat of the checkered vehicle and it whisked him away from the scene.

Tiaz stared out of the back window wearing a crinkled forehead and a tight jaw. *Yeahhhh, mothafucka, like I told you, payback is a bitch.* He nodded his head.

Bury Me A G 2

# Chapter Nine

Savon sat at the bar nursing a glass of Hennessy over the rocks. His homeboy, a dark skinned cat with three lines cut into the side of his fade, sat beside him on a bar stool facing the opposite direction. He tossed back beer nuts and watched a couple of patrons play pool. He ate the last beer nut and when he went to grab some more from the bowl on the bar top, he caught a glimpse of Savon's long face.

"What's eating you, my nigga?" the dark skinned cat asked.

Savon shook his head and said, "Nothing, Flaco, I'm straight, folks." He smacked the bar top signaling for the bartender to refill his glass.

"Bullshit, I know when my ace got something on his mind." Flaco said. "Speak on it, my ninja."

"My sister." Savon finally spat it out. "I don't see how she can be in love with this piece of shit. Nigga cheated on her, beat her ass, and now I find out that he had my nephew out here hustling. If I would have known he had them kids out there when we had'em that night, I would have shot that nigga dead in his mouth."

"It ain't too late." Flaco told him. "We can find him and string his buff ass up, do'em something nasty like Treach did old boy in Jason's Lyric."

"Nah." He shook his head. "It'll crush big sis' heart. That's the only reason why I'ma let this nigga keep his life. But God help me, if homie comes near either of them again, I'ma make good on my threat." He took a sip of his Hennessy.

Flaco patted his right hand on the shoulder and turned around to the bar on his stool. Still tossing back beer nuts, he addressed the bartender, "Nigel, let me get a Patron with lime."

A voluptuous woman, thick in all of the right places, stepped to the bar. She had a pretty face and an ass that would make a man want to saddle it for a ride. Her brownish red crown of curly hair flowed down her back. Her golden complexion shined under the dim lights of the establishment, setting off the glitter sprinkled over her chest and arms. She wore a black sweater over a white shirt that boasted her 36 double Ds. The black leather skirt that hugged her hips matched the six inch high heels that adorned her pedicured feet. Flaco was ogling the woman from head to toe, while Savon hadn't even so much as glanced her way. Now, normally another time and place, his homeboy would have been all over her, but his emotional state had him inebriated. Old girl could have been butt ass naked holding a condom and he wouldn't try to fuck her.

The bartender brought Flaco back his drink and he slowly sipped it, as he checked out the merchandise that was double D's body.

"I'd like a Sex on the Beach, thank you." Double D told the bartender.

"Coming right up." The bartender went about the task of making the drink.

Double D turned her soft brown eyes and hypnotizing smile on Savon, brushing a strand of hair behind her ear. "Hi, how are doing? I'm Lola." She introduced herself as she extended her manicured hand.

"Savon," he introduced himself as he shook her hand.

Seeing that Lola's sights were set on Savon, Flaco picked up his drink and excused himself. "I'ma go over here and probably shoot a few games of pool, man." He placed a hand on his homeboy's shoulder before wandered off.

"Alright," Savon told him. Then he turned to Lola. "So, where are you from, Ms. Lola?"

"Well, I'm originally from the Dominican Republic, but I moved from out there to New York and then here. I've been out here for about," she cut her eyes to the right as she tried to remember how long she'd been living in Los Angeles, "I'd say about four, four and a half years now."

Savon and Lola chopped it up for a couple of hours. Within that time they'd gotten to know a little about one another and started feeling each other. Lola paid for her drinks, as well as his. Every time he'd reach into his pocket to pay the tab she'd smack his hand down and drop a few bills to pay for the both of them. She laughed and giggled at all of his jokes whether they were funny or corny. Her company brought him out of his bad mood. He was in the presence of a beautiful woman and had to turn his charm on. He spat a little game and got her to agree to come back home with him.

"Hey, man, I'm outta here." Savon slapped hands with Flaco.

"You gone, huh?" Flaco smiled and took a sip of his drink, eying Lola who was on his best friend's arm. "I'm glad someone could get chu outta your funk."

"I'll holla." Savon said, making his exit from the establishment.

Savon stopped at the Arco gas station to fuel up and to let Lola use the rest room. He paid for the gas with his Visa credit card and stuck the pump into the gas tank slot of his Camero. He'd just turned his head to find Lola doing something in the backseat, his brows furrowed.

"What chu doing?"

"I think I lost my ID in here when I dropped my purse. I wanna get me a little bottle of something."

"Oh." He nodded.

"Here it is." Lola smiled, holding up her ID. She climbed out of the vehicle and slammed the door shut, strutting back toward the gas station's entrance. Savon cracked a smile as he admired her healthy ass.

"I'ma tear that big old ass up once we get back to the house." He made his plans out loud. "Yo, Lola," he called after her.

She stopped and turned around. "Yes."

"Grab me a bag of Doritos and a Coke."

"All right, Boo, I got chu." She sauntered into the Arco gas station.

Once Savon finished pumping the gas, he put the pump back into its premium 91 slot and hopped back into the car. He laid his head back against the headrest and rested his eyes for a time. Opening his eyes, he glanced at his watch, realizing that ten minutes had passed. He looked through the passenger side window into the Arco gas station and didn't see Lola inside. In fact, there wasn't any one inside save for the cashier, and he was leaning over the counter reading a magazine. Savon's forehead wrinkled and he wondered what was going on. He grabbed the door handle and made to get out of the car when a police cruiser came to a screeching halt behind him. He looked into the rearview mirror and saw the cop behind the wheel pick up the radio transceiver for the loud speaker.

"Driver, remove the keys from out of the ignition and toss them out of the window. I then want you to step out of your vehicle with your hands where I can see them." The voice boomed from the loud speaker.

"Man, this is some bullshit!" Savon cursed. He tossed his keys out of the window and stepped out of the car, with his hands up in surrender.

"Now get down on your knees with your back to me and place your hands on the top of your head." The voice boomed from the loud speaker once again.

Savon did like he was told. Two cops hopped out of the police cruiser with their guns drawn. One cuffed his hands behind his back and brought him to his feet, while the other searched the car.

"This is some bullshit, man! I'm getting tired of you mothafuckaz harassing me!" Savon barked as he was ushered towards the police cruiser. He had a banger in the car, but it was in a stash spot that he knew the police would never find. "Don't y'all have something better to do? Some real criminals to arrest or something? I'm just a hard working black man tryna keep my head above water!"

Savon was placed into the backseat of the police cruiser and the door was slammed on his ranting. He quieted down and watched the cops search his whip. His eyes bugged and his stomach twisted into knots when he saw one of the cops hold up a gun by its barrel, showing it to his partner. His partner took the gun and laid it on the hood of the police cruiser. The cop that discovered the gun inside of Savon's car reached back inside and came back out with a Macy's shopping bag. He walked the shopping bag over to the hood of the car and sat it down. He dipped his hand inside and pulled out two bricks of cocaine, both wrapped in cellophane. The cop placed the bricks back inside of the bag then looked at Savon through the windshield of the cruiser, smiling.

"What the fuck? That shit ain't mine!" Savon yelled. "That shit is not mine!"

At that moment, a black car pulled up beside the police cruiser. Savon looked to the passenger side's tinted window as it slowly rolled down, eventually revealing Lola's pretty face. She smiled and waved to Savon, enraging him.

"Fuck you, bitch! I'ma kill yo' fucking ass!" Savon barked, his hot breath fogging up the window glass. He hawked up phlegm and spat it on the window glass and it oozed down into the pane. Lola leaned back in the seat and Tiaz stuck his head into the window, smiling wickedly. "Mothafucka, you set me up! You fucking set me up!" Savon plopped down on his back and kicked the window glass until it cracked into a spider's web. Tiaz then pulled out of the gas station and away from the scene, leaving the cops to deal with Savon's temper tantrum.

Lola was Bianca, the same girl that Tiaz saw wrapped in the sheets in Threat's bed when he came home from prison. She was a beautiful woman with a mesmerizing body that could put any man under her spell. Tiaz knew that she could use what she had to get close to Savon and plant the gun and drugs in his whip. Lola put the bricks under the driver seat along with the banger that Tiaz used to kill Capone, Bleek and Silk. She'd done this while Savon was pumping gas, making an excuse about having to use the rest room at the nearby gas station. When she dipped off into the rest room she found the murder weapon and the coke in a shopping bag in the single stall. By the time she was coming back, he was about finished pumping the gas. She stepped inside of the gas station and placed a call to the police. The police had enough on Savon to lock him up for the rest of his life. He'd never see the outside world again.

## Chapter Ten
*A day later*

Chevy stood over the kitchen sink with her hands in the sudsy water, washing dishes. A Newport hung from between her thick lips. Once she finished washing off a plate, she sat it aside in the other side of the sink. After washing a few more plates and glasses, she shook the foam from her hands and took a hold of the cigarette, taking a few pulls and polluting the air with white clouds.

Hearing the telephone ring, she quickly washed her hands and dried them off with a towel. She picked the cordless phone up and glanced at the caller ID. The screen read: *Los Angeles County Facility*. Chevy's brows wrinkled, she wondered who could have been calling her from jail. She started to hang the phone up, but her curiosity got the best of her and she decided to answer it. She pressed *talk* and placed the phone to her ear. Once she finished listening to the operator and heard the person state their name, she pressed 1 to accept the call.

"Savon, what the hell are you doing in jail?" she inquired nervously.

"Come down here to see me, I need to talk to you," Savon responded in a grave tone.

"Fuck that, I'm bailing you out. How much is your bail?" She picked her purse up from off of the kitchen table and went through the big face Benjamin Franklins in her wallet, trying to see how much money she had to bail her baby brother out.

"I don't have a bail, Chevy. These crackas tryna lock your boy up and throw away the key. I may not ever see the light of day again," he stated sadly.

"Oh, my God, Savon, what did you do?" Chevy asked, devastated, placing a hand over her chest. Her eyes widened and her jaw dropped, the news was like a gut punch.

"I ain't do shit, girl, bring your ass down here." He told her. "This shit runs deep."

"Where are you?" she asked, filling a glass with water from under the faucet. She took a drink and wiped her mouth with the back of her hand.

"Central. You remember where it is, right?"

"Yeah, I've been there enough times. I'll be down there in a minute."

"All right. I love you," he said as an afterthought.

"I love you, too, and I'm finna come right now." She swore before hanging up, grabbing her purse and walking out the door, the dishes in the sink completely forgotten. She didn't have to worry about Te'Qui, because he was with his father. He'd taken him for the day to talk about the loss of his friend and him hustling out in the streets.

Once she was frisked and had her purse searched, Chevy was allowed entry into the visiting room. Her eyes went down the row of Plexiglass windows where the visitors were sitting on stools and talking on the telephones to their incarcerated loved ones who sat behind the glass. There was one vacant stool and behind the glass was Savon dressed in a navy blue jumpsuit and wearing a band around his wrists. Chevy sat down on the stool and picked up the telephone. When Savon picked up his telephone and placed it to his ear, she noticed his busted and bloody knuckles.

Chevy's forehead wrinkled seeing that her baby brother had gotten into some trouble inside. She wish she could come behind that glass and get with whatever bitch ass nigga that had a problem with him. She was his big sister, so it was natural for her wanting to take up for him, even though he was a grown ass man. It had always been that way between the two of them. Chevy had his back and Savon had hers.

"Bro, what happened to your hands?" she inquired.

Savon glanced at the knuckles of the hand he used to hold the telephone to his ear. It was as if he hadn't noticed that they were busted until Chevy had pointed it out to him. Even then it wasn't a big deal to him. He'd been behind the wall before and understood that fades and stabbings was the way of the land. You were either sheep or wolf. He was the latter and had no quarrels with baring his fangs.

"Oh, this ain't nothing." He shrugged like it wasn't a big deal. "I just had to give one of these bitch made ass niggaz in here some act right."

"So, what they got chu in here for?"

"Man, they found two bricks of yay and a strap with three bodies on it from a kick doe under the seat of my car."

"Damn, Savon." Chevy shook her head, hating to hear the bad news. "I thought you were done with the game?"

"I am. Yo' boyfriend planted that bullshit on me."

"Who?" she frowned.

"Tiaz and this Spanish bitch. He sent her to set me up. Now I'm fucked with a capital F." He shook his head with red webbed, glassy eyed, stressed out. He wasn't about to cry, but the thought of spending the rest of his life in prison was a mothafucka.

"Why would Tiaz have someone do this?" Lines ran across her forehead, with curiosity. She wanted to know exactly where her ex's place was in all of this.

"'Cause I had my boys beat his ass. I started to body him, but I didn't, thinking about you and your tender heart. If I would have done homeboy, I wouldn't be sitting in this shithole with cases up the ass. They're tryna bury your baby bro in here, Chevy. They wanna lock me under the jail."

"I'm not going to let that happen, okay?" she said with tears in her eyes. With the exception of Te'Qui, he was all she had. Her mind was already processing trying to figure out how to get her brother out of that shithole.

"Do you hear me? I'm not gonna let you rot in here. I'm gonna find a good lawyer and we're going to get chu outta here."

"That's what it's gonna take. A hell of a lawyer and a miracle from God, 'cause otherwise I'm washed up. I'm talking about the long haul. Life."

"I got your back, trust me." Tears ran down her cheeks.

"Listen, I'm going to need you to go to my crib." Savon told her. "There's a safe in the floor of my closet with more than enough trap for me a lawyer and to tie you and Te'Qui over. I want chu to get them ends and get me a solid attorney."

Chevy nodded. "Alright."

"The key to the house is under the welcome mat. The safe's combination is the last two numbers of mommy and daddy's birthday year."

"Okay."

Chevy made to get up, but Savon saying her name froze her midway. "Stay the fuck away from that nigga, Tiaz. He ain't no good for you and Te'Qui."

"Don't worry. After the shit he just put me through, I'm done." She placed her hand on the glass and he did, too. She then kissed it, leaving the imprint of her lipgloss behind. Chevy stood erect and walked away, determined to get her baby brother from behind the wall.

# Chapter Eleven

Threat sat behind the wheel of a Time Warner Cable van, tapping his fingers on the steering wheel and every so often glancing at the sideview mirror. His cell phone vibrated and he pulled it from his hip, looking at the screen.

*I told u 2 stop fuckn wit ma ppl. Now I'ma bust yo head! U r a dead man!*

Threat smirked as he read one of several of Don Juan's messages. He'd been sending them ever since he found out about them hitting Roots' people for that money. That, combined with all of the other times he and Tiaz had robbed his customers and the cats he was allied with, had him wanting them zipped up in black bags. Threat didn't give a fuck though. He punched a message into his cell phone. *Suck ma dick!!!* Then pressed *send*.

"Aye, Crim, this nigga, Don, on one." Threat said over his shoulder to Tiaz, who was in the back of the van putting on a Time Warner Cable uniform. Lying unconscious at his feet was the cable man zipcuffed and in his boxer briefs.

"Oh yeah? Fuck that nigga!"

"Old faggot ass salty about us hitting his people. You said you wanted to stick this nigga, right? Well, we're gone rob'em and leave'em lying face down. I know where all of his traps at and a couple of spots where he lays his head."

"Well, let's get it. That's a payday," Tiaz replied once he'd gotten dressed. He secured a head bussa inside of his jacket, slapped on a cap with the company logo emblazoned across it and buckled the utility belt across his waist. He then picked up the clipboard from off of the passenger seat and turned to his man. "Are you sure she's the only one there?" he asked about Kantrell's mother.

"The only people that live there is her and her son, but he's hardly ever there. If the nigga ain't lying up somewhere with a broad, then he's bussing tables at IHOP." Threat glanced at his watch. He was dressed in a cap with the Time Warner Cable logo emblazoned across it and the uniform as well. "It's 1 o'clock now, he's been at work for two hours."

"Alright," Tiaz hopped out of the van. Threat watched him through the windshield as he knocked on the door of a tan house. Kantrell's mother lived in poverty, a very shitty neighborhood off of Hooper Avenue, where fights, shootouts and loud music were a common thing. For the most part, everyone got along, because they minded their own business. Around this hour, residents were at work and their children were at school, while everyone else was up scheming on a dollar or already out on a paper chase.

The door cracked open and Tiaz talked with someone for a time before being let inside.

\*\*\*

"Alright, ma'am, your connection seems to be stable, now if you'll sign here I can gone and get out of your hair." Tiaz showed Kantrell's mother where to sign the document on the clipboard. Gaining entrance inside of her house was as easy as he thought it would be. He tampered with the wiring on the line and disrupted her service. The bugs Threat had planted when he was spying on Kantrell were still intact, so they knew when she made the call. Once she put it through, they paid a smoker to call right back and cancel.

Kantrell's mother signed on the line marked with an X. When she went to hand the clipboard back to him he was mad dogging her and pointing his steel at her face. Her eyes bugged and her jaw slackened. She dropped the clipboard and placed her hand over her heart. "Where's Kantrell?"

"I, I don't know." She stammered.

"Wrong answer." Tiaz jabbed her in the eye with the barrel of his gun, causing her to yelp in pain. She grabbed her eye and staggered backwards, wincing. When she took her hand from her eye, it was swollen and discolored.

"I swear I don't know where she is. I haven't spoken to her in months,"she shouted.

Tiaz picked up the cordless telephone and checked the caller ID. There was a call from *Kantrell Combs*. The most recent call was dated for that day.

"You lying..." He was cut short by a lamp flying at his head. He dodged the lamp and it shattered against the wall. Kantrell's mother went running past him, screaming for help. She headed into the kitchen, closing in for the back door. Once she unlocked the door, she then unlocked the iron security door behind it. When she pulled the iron door open, Threat swung into the doorway, punching her dead in the face. She fell to the floor on her back, unconscious. He pulled the door closed behind him and locked it. Tiaz tucked his thang thang on his waistline. He grabbed her by her arms and dragged her back into the living room, where he duct taped her to a chair.

He tried smacking her back conscious, but she wouldn't come to. He then filled up a bucket of water and poured it on her head. She came to gasping for air. She looked from Tiaz's scowl to Threat's, feeling like a mouse trapped in the corner of a cage by a viper. She screamed for help again and Threat cracked her in the forehead with the butt of his gun. Blood rolled down her forehead and got into her eye, she looked like she was about to faint until he smacked her viciously across the face. The assault stung and left a red hand impression on her cheek.

"Scream again and it'll be the last thing you do." He threatened with a steady, calm voice. She could see in his eyes that she was wearing on his nerves and he wouldn't hesitate to carry out his namesake *threat*. "Now, where is Kantrell? And don't lie to me." He turned to Tiaz. "Yo' turn the TV on and crank the volume. I don't nobody to hear us in here."

Tiaz nodded and did as he was instructed.

Kantrell's mother closed her eyes and tried to get her head together before speaking. "I spoke to Trell earlier, but she didn't tell me where she was. She was just calling to see how I was doing, since we haven't spoken to each another in a while."

"That's it? She didn't say where she was calling from or where she was going?" Threat asked.

"No, she didn't." She shook her head no.

"Oh, alright." Threat said coolly. He then turned to Tiaz. "Go into the kitchen and see what you can find flammable, T, I'ma 'bout to barbeque this bitch."

The buff neck thug rose from the arm of the couch and went to carry out Threat's order. Kantrell's mother started screaming at the top of her lungs, but there wasn't any use, because that loud ass TV masked her shrills. Pissed off, Threat cracked her across the jaw, nearly knocking her unconscious. He then tore off a strip of duct tape and sealed her mouth shut with it.

Tiaz returned from the kitchen and handed him a tin can of charcoal fluid. He squirted the fluid all over her face and body. He sat the can down on the coffee table and turned back around to her as she was coming to. He pulled out a book of matches and struck a flame with one of the sticks.

When she saw the burning match and smelled the charcoal fluid on her person, she screamed as loud as she could, but the noise was muffled by the duct tape over her mouth. She whipped her head back and forth and thrashed around in the chair as he brought the burning match near her, smiling fiendishly.

*Heavenly Father, what has this child of mine gotten me into with these men she's been dealing with? Lord have mercy, she done brought these devils right upon my doorstep. And if I don't give 'em what they want, they are sure to burn me at the stake,* she thought, shaking her head, shamefully. *Kantrell is always in some shit. I can't help her this time, she done put my life in danger now. Selfish ass done left me out here to suffer the consequences of her actions. Well, I'm not gon' do it, Jeffery, forgive me.* She looked up at the ceiling talking to her late husband, *but I refuse to give my life away knowing once I'm gone our baby girl will continue living the way she does.*

"You ready to talk now?" he asked. She nodded yes and he ripped the strip of tape from her mouth, leaving a red bruise behind. She winced after having the tape ripped from her mouth. He fanned out the flame from the match stick and tossed it aside.

"Where is she?" As she spilled the details on her daughter's whereabouts, Threat mentally recorded the vital information to his memory. Once she finished forwarding her daughter's information, he gave a nod to Tiaz who was behind her. She went to look over her shoulder, but before she could turn her head all the way around, a bullet exited out of her forehead. Her chin fell to her chest and blood dripped from the gaping hole in her dome.

A dead woman tells no tales!

Bury Me A G 2

# Chapter Twelve

Kantrell sat at the dining table inside of the hotel room she'd rented for the week. A smile was plastered on her face as she ran stacks of cash through the money counting machine and took pulls from a cigarette. Once the machine was done counting the money, she'd dip her hand back into the briefcase for another stack and dropped it into the slot. She'd smile and lick her lips in delight as the cash rapidly shuffled before her eyes. She felt moisture building between her legs as the Benjamin Franklins were flickered through the counter. Sex was always good, but it was the money that made her cum.

"Cash makes the coochie woo, woo." She cracked a smile, sounding like Cookie from *Next Friday*.

Kantrell had taken a liking to Tiaz. He had a pretty good up and down game. He knew her body like the back of his hand. It was like he had the blueprint to making her orgasm in his mind. His stroke took her to another plane of existence, where pleasure and pain lived in harmony. She came harder than she'd ever come, but a nut was just a nut. Good dick was scarce and hard to come by, but to hell with it, she had a vibrator. Some people never touch two million dollars in their lifetime. Hell, the average Joe was lucky if a million passed through his hands, let alone two. So when she had to choose between a blossoming romance with Tiaz and that loot, she chose the money without a second thought. In her mind cash couldn't replace love, but it was a damn good substitute.

It never even crossed Kantrell's mind how she'd purposely went after her best friend's man, got him, ended their friendship and then dropped him like it was no big deal, all for a shit load of cash.

"Fuck the both of them, a bitch got money." She blew smoke from her nose and mouth as if she didn't have a care in the world.

This was Kantrell's fifth time counting the money. Every time she totaled the amount on her calculator, she couldn't believe the numbers staring back at her. $1,995,000 dollars. Seeing the number this time made her giddy and she screamed like a teenage girl after being asked out by her crush. Kantrell picked up her cell phone and scrolled down her contacts until she found the number she was looking for. *Work.* Once she pressed *call,* she placed the cell phone to her ear. She mashed her square out into the ashtray and cleared her throat, preparing herself to speak.

"Hello, may I speak with Ms. Morgan please? Kantrell Combs," she said into the cell real proper like. "Batice, what's cracking you beady eyed, beaver teeth, lace front wearing, swap meet jewelry rocking bitch? I was just calling to tell yo' bitter ass that I quit! Fuck you and that punk ass job! Now choke on that dick!"

"Choke on what? You got me…"

Kantrell hung up before Ms. Morgan could finish her rebuttal, laughing her ass off. She went about the task of stacking the money back into the briefcases. Once she placed the last stack inside of the briefcase, she placed them safely inside the closet. She grabbed the bottle of Rose from out of the refrigerator and popped the top on it. The foam ran over her knuckles and she took the bottle to the head like it was a 40 oz of St. Ides malt liquor. She brought the bottle down from her lips and wiped her mouth with the back of her hand. She then poured some into a champagne flute. She watched the foam rise to the top before taking another sip.

Kantrell heard someone knocking at the door. She was about to retrieve her Glock .23 from where it was wedged between the cushions of the couch, but remembered she'd asked the cleaning lady to bring her clean linen. Once she grabbed a few bucks from out of her pocket book for a tip, she headed for the door. She took a glance through the peep hole and confirmed that it was the cleaning lady. Seeing that it was her, she turned the knob and pulled the door open. The cleaning lady was holding a stack of folded linen. She had long thick curly hair and wore glasses. Her eyes had a murderous glint to them and her face was lighter than her natural tan. It was obvious that this impostor was wearing makeup. Once it registered in Kantrell's head that it wasn't the old Cuban lady standing before her, but Threat disguised as her, she felt her bladder fill and urine threatening to spill down her legs.

Hidden beneath the linen in Threat's hand was a black banger. Threat punched Kantrell in the face and sent her sailing back. She tried to grab a hold of something to stop from falling, but ended up grabbing air on the way down. He stepped into the room and tossed the linen from his hands, exposing the ebony gun with the silencer attachment. He closed the door behind him, all the while keeping an eye on Kantrell as she made to get upon her feet. She got up on one knee and brought her hand upon the wall. Threat aimed his banger and pulled the trigger, sending a bullet through her hand. The bullet tore through the bones and tendons in her mitt and lodged itself into the wall.

"Rarrrhhh!" Kantrell's face twisted in agony. When she took her hand from the wall, there was a red smear. She tucked her mangled hand in her armpit and made to get up again, but a hot one through the back of her kneecap brought her back down to the floor. She yelped and hit the carpet, wearing a mask of excrucitation as tears rolled from the corners of her eyes.

Threat approached her, stomping her in the stomach and kicking her in the spine, drawing a wail that sounded like it would have came from a wounded walrus.

"Bitch, you thought you were gonna get away with my mothafucking money?" He kicked her in the head and then in the ear, setting off an eerie siren and causing her eyes to bulge. She grabbed for his leg as he assaulted her, but it didn't do any good. He continued to kick and stomp her until his chest was heaving and he was out of breath. "Where are my chips, huh? What chu do with my paper?" he asked, while he gripped the back of her neck and held the head bussa in her mouth.

She heard him, but she was in too much pain to say anything. Seeing that he wasn't going to get an answer out of Kantrell, Threat kicked her in the ribs and stormed into the bedroom, returning moments later with the briefcases of money. A smile was plastered on his face as he traveled back down the hall. Returning to the living room, he saw Kantrell crawling towards the couch. He sat the briefcases down and whipped out his gun. Just as he extended it to the back of her skull, she swung around holding the Glock .23, squeezing the trigger rapidly. Each shot propelled Threat further back across the living room, with his face twisting in pain. He collapsed to the floor on his back, grimacing and kicking his right leg.

Kantrell hobbled over to the briefcases. She tried to pick up both of the briefcases, but her left hand wasn't worth a damn. *Damn! I hate to leave one, but what choice do I have?* She dropped the Glock into the briefcase, closed it and grabbed it by the handle, hobbled her way over to the door, opened it and made her way out.

Threat ripped open the cleaning lady's uniform and felt under the bulletproof vest he had on. He winced as his hand brushed over the sore areas of his chest and ribs. Had it not been for the Kevlar, he would have found out if there was a heaven for a gangster. He got to his feet as mad as a hornet, picked up his weapon and ran out of the door just in time to see Kantrell's back as she limped down the hallway. He aimed that thang at her back and pulled the trigger, but the gun jammed. He examined the head bussa trying to right it, but he couldn't get it in working order. Seeing a fire-axe encased in a glass box, he used the butt of his gun to shatter the glass. He tucked the banger on his waistline and pulled the axe free from its confines then went after his prey with madness in his eyes that made him resemble Jack Nicholson in The Shining.

Fuck the money, he wanted that bitch's life bad! So bad that he didn't give a shit about the surveillance cameras monitoring the halls. His rage had consumed him and he'd completely lost it. He was driven mad, mad with vengeance.

"I'm gonna kill you, bitch!" he roared, eyes looking like embers, he was so hot. "I'm gonna fucking chop you up into little pieces!" Spit flew from off of his lips as he sprinted down the corridor, quickly closing up the distance.

Kantrell could feel someone behind her as she limped down the hall. She looked over her shoulder and saw Threat coming at her, wielding an axe. The sight of him brought a chill up her spine and fueled the will in her to live. She limped forth as fast as she could on one leg. Seeing the stairwell exit door at her right added to her stamina and drove her to push harder. She felt excitement rise inside of her the closer she got to the stairwell door. The hairs stood up on her neck when she felt Threat on top of her, his hot breath moistening the back of her neck. She had just reached the stairwell door when she saw his silhouette on the floor as he swung the axe. She ducked the swing of the deadly weapon and it stabbed into the corridor's wall. As he struggled to pry it loose, she went through the stairwell door. Once he pulled the axe free, he made to go after her, but the shouting coming from down the hall halted him.

"Freeze, drop the axe!"

Threat looked up and saw two police officers with their guns drawn on him. He weighed his options. He could still try to go after Kantrell and risk being shot, or he could surrender and take his chances on trial. Figuring that he'd rather be judged by twelve than carried by six, he tossed the axe aside and put his hands up in the air. He was ordered down on his knees with his hands behind his head. The police officers moved in on him. One of them handcuffed him then ordered his partner to check the room where the gunshots were reported from.

***

Tiaz sat parked across the street from the Ritz hotel with his eyes glued on the entrance, smoking a cigarette. He looked alive when he saw two police officers escorting Threat out of the hotel in handcuffs. Heated, he cursed and dipped his hand inside of the console, withdrawing a banger. He clicked the safety off and made to hop out when he saw Threat look him dead in the eyes and shake his head. Tiaz wanted to say fuck it and bang it out with the law and help his friend escape. Although he knew he'd be jeopardizing his own life, he was still willing to risk it. Threat was his man, one hundred grand. There wasn't anything that he wouldn't do for him, and vice versa. They were down for each another and all they had was each other.

Reluctantly, Tiaz settled back down in his seat watching as Threat was put in the backseat of the police cruiser and driven away. He figured that his head was in the right place. He was looking at a third strike, which meant life imprisonment, so he'd need him out on the streets to get up some paper for a lawyer, if he was going to have a chance at beating his charge. Tiaz resurrected the engine of the stolen Ford Explorer and pulled off, thinking on how his life had spiraled out of control.

\*\*\*

Kantrell made her way down the staircase, dripping blood as she went along. Once she reached the last landing, she tore off the end of her blouse and ripped it in half. She used one half to tie around her hand and the other to tie around her leg to slow the bleeding. She then picked the briefcase up and pushed open the door that led out into the lobby, where she made a left and headed out the back exit.

As soon as she pushed open the back exit door, she was overwhelmed by the fluorescent rays of the sun. Its illumination was so intense that it caused her to narrow her eyes into slits as she made her way through the parking lot. Once her eyes got adjusted to the sun, she was able to carry herself over to her Buick Lasabre with no problem. She unlocked the vehicle, hopped into the driver seat and sat the briefcase on the floor on the passenger side. She drove out of the parking lot and made a left, traveling down a residential street. Kantrell steered the car as best as she could with her left arm, while she used her right hand to search through the ashtray until she found a roach. She put it between her lips and pressed the car lighter in. Once it popped out, the tip of it glowed amber it was so hot. She went to bring the lighter to the end of the roach when something slammed into the side of her. The force was so great that it sent her Buick Lasabre spinning and smashing into a parked car.

Kantrell brought her head up and looked around in a daze. She saw two men hop out of a red Ford F-150 pick-up truck. They wore matching red bandanas over the lower halves of their faces. Their gloved hands were wrapped around black Uzis. Her mouth went dry and her heart raged inside of her chest. A panic alarm rang inside of her head, telling her she'd better put up a defense to protect her life.

She reached down over the passenger seat, popped the locks on the briefcase and picked up her Glock. She went to lift the gun and sprays of automatic gunfire came from both sides of her. The rush of bullets came in and out of her from all angles, decorating the inside of her car with splatters of blood and broken glass. Her head lay against the headrest. She stared up at the ceiling looking through blurry eyes. Her chest heaved up and down, as she fought against the darkness that tried to procure her. She saw one of the Uzi toting men use the butt of his weapon to knock out the shards of glass that lined the window. She watched as he reached inside of the busted out window to open the door, but she was too weak to stop him.

The man opened the door, grabbed Kantrell by her blouse and pulled her out onto the sidewalk. He looked over to his partner and he was pulling the briefcase out of the car from the opposite side. He took a peek inside of the briefcase and gave him a nod, letting him know that the money was there. He then set his sights on Kantrell. He tilted his head to the right as he watched her gasp for air. He'd killed many people in his lifetime and he always wondered what went through their minds while they were dying. He didn't know the answer to that question, and he hoped to remain ignorant for many years to come.

Kantrell knew this would be her final moments alive, she saw her life flash before her eyes. She never thought that her choices would come back to harm her like this, damn! Her eyes welled up with tears and distorted her vision, realizing she was going to be left to die alone on the streets like a wounded animal. She regretted some of the trifling things she'd done and the many things that she didn't live long enough to do.

"Gaaahgaggg." She choked on her own blood, tears steadily streaming down her cheeks. "Please. Please God. Save. Save me. I promise I'ma do right. I promise to, gagg, haaaa, live my life. Righteously." She strained to say those last words. Red streams ran from the corners of her mouth and made small pools at her head. She then closed her eyes and waited for a miracle to happen. It didn't come though. Instead she got bullets.

*Blurraaaaat!*

He swept his Uzi across Kantrell's chest, killing her instantly. Then he hopped back into the passenger seat of the F-150 truck, while his partner walked over to a Cadillac ATS that had just rolled up. The dark tinted window of the driver side slowly rolled down and revealed Smack's face. The man handed him the briefcase through the window. He took a brief glance inside then gave the man a nod. The man hopped back behind the wheel of the F-150 truck and drove away.

Smack pulled into a McDonald's parking lot and killed the engine of his Cadillac. He pulled a locator device out of his coat's pocket and looked at its screen. A red dot was flashing at the center of it. He then tore open the inside of the briefcase and removed a device that resembled a small cell phone. On its screen was a green dot that flashed like a blip on a radar scanner inside of a submarine. The small device was a tracker. Smack had planted them inside both of the briefcases so he'd be able to hunt down the people that had kidnapped his son. He turned off the tracker and dropped it inside of the briefcase. The red dot disappeared on the screen of the locator and he slipped it back into his coat's pocket.

\*\*\*

Threat rode in the backseat of the police cruiser, scrunched up and uncomfortable. The handcuffs were so tight on his wrists that he felt them cutting off his circulation, but he didn't bother to voice his grievance with the officer that had arrested him, because he knew it wouldn't do any good. He'd probably just tighten the handcuffs and make things even worse for him. For now, he was going to ignore the pain in his wrists, and enjoy what would probably be his last tour of the streets for a long time to come. Threat stared out of the window until he began to drift off. He struggled to keep a float, but eventually succumbed to sleep. Hearing the doors of the police cruiser slamming, he began to come to, looking around. He was in the woods. Realizing where he was, he looked alive.

"Aye, where the fuck y'all taking me, man?" Threat yelled out to the police officers. The shorter and heavier one of the officers opened the back door and pulled him out. He shoved him up against the police cruiser then drew his gun on him. His partner was right beside him drawing iron of his own. He tensed at first. Then he glared at the men before him, giving Death the middle finger.

"You don't know who we are, do you?" The taller and darker of the police officers asked, wearing a grin. Threat narrowed his eyes into slits, trying to remember where he'd seen the police officer before. Nothing clicked in his head until the police officer pulled off his afro wig and bushy mustache, tossing them aside.

"Don Juan." Threat frowned and sneered.

The shorter police officer removed his dark shades and threw them aside, turning his light brown eyes on Threat. His facial expression was less than friendly when he locked eyes with the short killer. They were mad dogging one another like a couple of riled up pit bulls that couldn't wait to be let loose from their leashes so they could lock ass.

"It's you, even without the cornrows and glasses. I could pick you outta line up." Faison said.

"Old boy from the hospital," Threat recalled.

"Yeah, that was my baby sister you tried to rock to sleep." He told him. "Fuck was that about?"

"Bitch dogged out my man. He's family, and family gets down for one another." Threat said like it was no big deal, spitting on the ground and shrugging. Tiaz was his mothafucking man and he'd lock ass with God Almighty behind him. That's just how loyal he was.

"I hope it was worth your life." Faison told him.

"That and more," Threat replied. His loyalty and love for Tiaz was unbreakable. If he'd asked him to go on a mission to hell to assassinate the Devil, he'd do it without a second thought. You couldn't buy a friend like Threat with a briefcase full of money.

Hearing a vehicle's engine and the snapping of twigs, Don Juan spared a glance over his shoulder and saw a red Ford F-150 pulling up. Bird and Bone hopped out of the truck and approached the trio. Faison heard the engine of a car to his right. He turned around to find a silver Mercedes Benz. The driver side door swung open and Majestic stepped out, sucking on the end of a pipe. He closed the car door and started in the direction where everyone was gathered.

"I tried to warn your ass, Threat, but you just wouldn't listen." Don Juan shook his head. "I told you, stop sticking up my people, but chu wasn't trying to hear me. We were making good money, living it up."

"Fuck you!" Threat spat. "I don't answer to anybody, but my mothafucking self! I get mine behind a ski mask and the trigger of a gun! If fuck niggaz don't lay it down, then they get put down! If we aren't homies or fam, then I'm coming after your ass for that check! Ain't no exemptions! Y'all take me where my life is to end. This nigga is getting on my fucking nerves!"

"Y'all heard the man," Majestic said. "Let's get going."

The night was dark and cold. The only thing that could be heard in the distance was an owl and the occasional howling wolf. The men trekked on through the sticks. Every time they took a breath, white smoke appeared. Threat was led to a pre-dug hole out in the middle of the woods. A lantern illuminated the hole and two shovels stood up in the piles of dirt beside it. He peeked over into the hole and when he turned back around Faison and Don Juan's guns were staring him in the face.

"Can a real nigga get his final request 'fore he leaves this bitch?" he asked.

"Go ahead." Don Juan told him.

"Let me blow one before y'all send me off." Threat looked between Faison and Don Juan. Bird took the blunt from behind his ear and put it between his lips. He then whipped out a Bic lighter and set the end of it ablaze. Threat took a few puffs and blew out smoke. Don Juan allowed him to smoke it halfway down, before he took it out of his mouth and threw it to the ground. He mashed it out under his boot heel and stepped back next to Faison with his gun trained on Threat.

For a time they just stood there with their guns held on him, not uttering a word, trying to see if he'd break down and beg for his life. Not a chance. Threat looked between the two of them. His heart was beating fast, not because he was scared of dying, but because he wondered what death had in store for him.

"Fuck y'all waiting for? Send me to thug heaven." He told them. Faison and Don Juan unloaded on him. Their guns sounded like firecrackers and the ends of their weapons flickered with light. He danced on his feet as the bullets entered his front and exited his back. The gunfire ceased and smoke wafted in the air. He fell backwards into the hole dug specifically for him. The front of his cleaning uniform looked like it had been shot up with a barrage of red paint balls. Faison approached the end of the hole and stared down at his limp body. He dropped his banger inside of the hole and Don Juan dropped his in also. They stepped aside and allowed Bird and Bone to grab the shovels to bury Threat's body.

Los Angeles, California is a small place. If the people there didn't know someone then they knew someone that knew their people, and vice versa. Majestic and Smack used to run together back in the day. Majestic was Faison's cocaine plug and Smack was Don Juan's Godfather. Faison and Don Juan ran in some of the same circles. All of them had come under one umbrella to go against a common threat: Tiaz and Threat. Each man had an army of killers under his command and more than enough paper between them. With them united, Tiaz and Threat didn't stand a chance.

Once Threat was buried, everyone headed for their vehicles to leave. All of the men had hopped into their respective cars and left the woods, except Majestic. He'd just opened the driver side door of his Mercedes Benz and slid in behind the wheel.

"It's hot in here," Majestic said toTJ.

"I turned on the heater, it's cold outside," he responded. "My fucking legs ache when it's chilly, unc. You know that. Did they get Tiaz?"

"Nah, he wasn't with old dude, but don't worry, we'll get that sucka." Majestic said, resurrecting the Mercedes and driving off.

# Chapter Thirteen

Tiaz sat at the edge of the bed inside of his cheap, roach infested motel room, taking a fifth of Hennessy to the head. He was in deep thought as he wondered what had happened to Threat. He'd looked him up on the LASD.org website to see what he'd been locked up for, but there wasn't any record of him being taken into custody. He thought that was odd since he'd seen him being arrested with his own eyes. He knew for a fact that The Boys had gotten him. He even called around to different precincts asking if they had him. When they claimed to not have him, he put in calls to every hospital he could think of, figuring that he had gotten out of line and the police had beaten the shit out of him and that's why he hadn't been put in the LASD database yet.

Tiaz sat his bottle of Hennessy on the nightstand beside the old ass box shaped television set. He peeled the dressing off of the bullet wound he'd gotten, thanks to Te'Qui. He cleaned around the wound and added a fresh dressing to it. He then wrapped the surgical tape around it. Tiaz picked the bottle up from the nightstand and took it to the dome one more time, before grabbing one of the three duffle bags he'd brought. He sat the duffle bag on the bed and unzipped it. One at a time, he picked up a stack and counted it before setting it aside. When he finished he had counted $175,000 dollars. It was all of the money he had in the world. To most it would have been a nice little chunk of change, but he was used to having much more.

At one point in time, he had a safe with two million dollars in it. He saw it all from robbing and stealing. He got on his grind with that ski mask and that banger and touched the town. He put the muscle on every D-boy and two bit hustler that was handling. It got to the point where mothafuckas got tired of him robbing them and agreed to pay taxes in order to get their hustle on without any trouble. For a time, everything was sweet. Tiaz didn't even have to bust his gun anymore. He'd put that bitch on the shelf. All he was doing then was picking up his money from the taxes. It was all good until Tim Dog had to go and rob his bitch. That led to him jamming his ass up and catching that five year stretch. He hated himself for ever having busted his banger behind Ta'shauna's trifling ass, but it was nothing he could do about it now. What was done was done.

Tiaz placed the money back inside of the duffle bag and dropped it down in the closet. He then picked up the bottle of Hennessy and took a swallow. As he was placing it back on the nightstand, his cell phone rang with a generic ring tone, dancing across the dresser. Tiaz picked the cell phone up from the dresser and looked at the screen. *Threat* was flashing on it. His forehead wrinkled. He pressed *talk* and placed the cell phone to his ear.

"Threat?" Tiaz spoke into his cell.

"Nah, this ain't Threat, nigga."

Tiaz recognized the voice instantly, his face twisted with rage. "Faison?"

"That's right, Super Thug, turn on the TV," he told him. "Channel 11."

Tiaz picked the remote control up from the dresser and turned on the old TV set. He flipped through the channels until he reached eleven.

*Kantrell M. Combs was gunned down gangland style just a few blocks from the Ritz hotel. A witness reported to have seen two masked men hop out of a red pickup truck and open fire on Kantrell's vehicle with automatic weapons. Kantrell was then pulled out of the car and shot multiple times in the chest. We were told that one of the masked men took some-*

*thing from out of the vehicle before hopping into the pickup truck and leaving the scene...* The Asian reporter went on to disclose more information, but Tiaz ignored her. He focused his attention back on his conversation with Faison.

*Gutta snipe hoe lucky he got to that ass before I did. Good fucking riddance,* he harped up a glob of saliva and spit it at the TV. It spattered against the screen and slid downward, resting in the bottom outline of the television set.

"Yeah, that skeeza is somewhere in whore heaven about now," Faison continued. "And if you're wondering where your man, Threat, is, rest assured that nigga's dead. But don't trip, you'll be chilling with him soon enough. You touched my baby sister and now you die!" he growled.

"Sister?" Tiaz frowned, not knowing who he was talking about. Then it dawned on him and his eyes widened, *Ta'shauna.* His face quickly tightened with rage. *Now I wish Threat would have really off'd that bitch! Myself, Chevy, Te'Qui, Faison, Ta'shauna, we're all connected in one way or another. I guess it's true about this being a small world!*

"That's right. Ta'shauna Reed," Faison said, causing Tiaz' heart to skip a beat. He couldn't believe Ta'shauna and Faison were siblings. As far as he knew she didn't have any siblings. *Faison had to have been the cat that Threat had run into when he went to finish Ta'shauna. But how did Faison know that Threat was Ta'shauna's shooter? Threat had to have said something to her about me before he blasted that bitch,* Tiaz thought. It didn't matter, because Faison was Tiaz' to deal with now. And he was going to handle him accordingly. "You moved on my family, now both of you niggaz are getting touched."

"Check this out," Tiaz began. "Fuck you, fuck your sister, and fuck your family! All y'all can eat a dick! You fucked up, homes! You hit the kill switch on a real beast!

I'm banger'd up, trigga happy and ain't got nothing to lose! I'm finna get off the chain, pussy!" He hung up the cell phone and tossed it on the nightstand.

He plopped down on the bed, removing the cork from the Hennessy bottle. He took a deep breath and guzzled the dark liquor down. The liquid coated his belly and ignited a fire inside of him, causing him to hiss like a snake.

"Damn, Threat." Tiaz shook his head, hating his brother from another had gotten his cap twisted. The effects of the liquor were welcoming, especially after the news he was just given. The only person in the world that gave a damn if he was breathing or not had been murdered. It never came to mind that others cared about him, but his callous disregard and mistreatment had alienated those people. Tiaz's eyes became red webbed and glassy. He was hurting. His insides felt like they were rotting and crumbling like an ancient Chinese temple. With Threat gone there wasn't anything for him to live for. His death was a mothafucka, but it gave Tiaz an excuse to show his ass. The tools he had on deck were going to give his enemy a taste of his pain and turmoil. This would be the way he mourned. It was the only way he knew how, because he couldn't see tears coming down his face.

\*\*\*

Faison rolled Ta'shauna in a wheelchair down the hallway, accompanied by Bird and Bone. Ta'shauna had been released from Cedar Sinai hospital. Faison was going to put her up at his place with a couple of his guys to watch over her. He knew that she wasn't safe as long as Tiaz was alive. He'd dusted off his homeboy, so he knew that he would be on the prowl for revenge.

Faison had done his homework on him and found out that he was definitely someone he didn't want to take lightly. He'd heard stories about Tiaz that would have the average man shook, but Faison wasn't the average man. He was far from pussy. Not to mention he had clout, money and plenty of guns surrounding him. Hell, the way he figured, Tiaz was one man, while he had numbers on his side. One man could only hope to survive the army of gunners he had at his disposal.

"Did you do like I asked?" Faison said to Bone.

"Yeah," Bone answered. "We got both of them thangs bulletproofed, the Mercedes truck and the Maybach. I drove the Maybach up here today."

"Good, good." Faison nodded. "We gotta keep our eyes and ears open. He's only one dude, but that's all it really takes to do some damage. From what I've heard this mothafucka don't play, so I wanna be cocked, locked and ready to rock with his big diesel ass, you understand?"

Bone nodded. "I got chu, Bossman, don't worry. We're gonna get this cock sucka. We already done cliqued up with these other cats, so he's gotta deal with three other armies besides ours."

Faison rolled Ta'shauna through the automatic doors. As they approached the Maybach, Bird hopped out from the driver side and walked around to help them with Ta'shauna. Bone opened the backseat door. He and Faison moved to help Ta'shauna from her wheelchair when they heard someone calling Faison's name. Faison looked up and saw his mother, father and Uncle Bruce approaching from across the parking lot. He and Bone stopped with their dealing of Ta'shauna and turned to them, just as they stepped up on the curb.

"Are you taking her to our house?" Gloria asked Faison.

"Nah, ma, Tee's going to stay with me for a lil' while," Faison said. "She said she'll feel safer where I am. You and Uncle Bruce are welcome to come along if you want." His eyes darted to his father, letting him know that he wasn't stepping a foot inside of his home. Faison wasn't about to tell his mother that he had some cat gunning for him and most likely Ta'shauna. She'd urge him to contact the police, but he wasn't about to run to L.A's Finest. This was a street beef and he would deal with the matter accordingly.

"I'd like to go, but only if your father can come along," Gloria told Faison. She wanted to go along to help her daughter recover, but she wanted her husband right there beside her. She only hoped that her only son would finally come to his senses and allow his father back inside of his home and his life.

Faison shook his head. "Ma, that man didn't want me in his house, so I for damn sure don't want him in mine."

"Junior, you and your father need to put this senseless feud behind you and..." Gloria was cut short when a bullet flew through her temple, killing her instantly and splattering blood on Faison's face. Automatic gunfire filled the air. Faison stood frozen stiff.

Everything seemed to move in slow motion as he looked around in awe. Hot lead tore through his family and both of his henchmen. The air was sprayed with crimson mists as bullets flew in and out of his loved ones, hitting vital organs and tearing off some of their limbs. Their mortal screams and cries flooded his ear drums and he felt like he was in the middle of a war zone. He looked over his shoulder and saw a masked man holding a Steyr Aug, firing away as if he were on the set of a Rambo movie. The masked man whipped the German machine gun around in Ta'shauna's direction. Seeing his sister in direct danger, lit a fire under Faison's ass.

He had to get to her before she was taken out of his life forever.

He jetted after her running as fast as he could, silently praying he reached her before death could.

"Shaunaaaaa!" he called out, moving like Marion Jones.

Just as Tiaz was squeezing the trigger, Faison was leaping into the air and tackling his sister's wheelchair to the ground. A bullet entered his leg as he crossed the line of fire.

*Ping! Ring! Ting!* The other rush of bullets narrowly missed him, sparking off of the metal of the wheelchair. The husky coke peddler yelled out in excruciation, clutching at his leg as he rolled off of Ta'shauna. He turned his eyes on the masked man as he approached, clutching his German machine gun. Faison tried to help Ta'shauna to her feet, but the masked man was closing in fast. Figuring there wasn't any use of both of them ending up dead, he hopped into the backseat of the Maybach and slammed the door closed.

The masked man had just run upon the door, pulling at its handle. He tried to open the door, but it was locked. Angry, he punched the tinted window and stepped back, gripping his machine gun and squeezing the trigger. The weapon rattled off hitting up the backseat window and leaving scratches behind. The bulletproofing had saved Faison's life. The masked man ran upon the Maybach and pointed his machine gun down at the sunroof. He blazed at the black tint, but only managed to scratch the surface.

"Fuck me," he cursed before jumping down onto the curb. He looked around on the ground and saw something that sparked his interest. Ta'shauna. He sat the wheelchair up and planted her in it. Tears slid down Ta'shauna's cheeks and she trembled uncontrollably. She was blind, and although she couldn't see the masked man's face, his aura was all she needed to confirm that he was Tiaz.

Tiaz pressed his weapon to Ta'shauna's temple. She closed her eyes and bit down on her bottom lip, silently praying that he didn't kill her. "Climb your hoe ass out from the backseat, or I'ma blast this bitch's skull apart!" he barked, with white stuff forming at the corners of his mouth. When Faison didn't hop right out, Tiaz pressed the barrel of his weapon further into Ta'shauna's temple, saying, "I'm gonna give you until the count of five! One...four..." The backseat door cracked open and an evil smile appeared on Tiaz's face. He turned his weapon on the open door as soon as Faison planted his foot down on the pavement. "Yeah, bring your ass on out..." he chuckled and smiled. He was about to get his revenge.

"Freeze, mothafucka!" a voice roared at Tiaz's back. He slowly turned his head to look over his shoulder. A police officer was standing inside of the hospital hall with his gun trained on Tiaz's back. Tiaz whipped his machine gun around and cut loose with a burst of flames. The police officer dove to the floor, avoiding the weapon as it spat fire. Four more police officers spilled out of the elevator, but they got out of dodge once Tiaz spat flames their way. The sounds of police sirens flooding the air and an approaching helicopter brought Tiaz's attention back around. He looked to Ta'shauna's wheelchair and it was vacant. He looked to the back door of the Maybach and it had just closed. Pissed off, he kicked the wheelchair over and shot up the rear window, before running off.

"Are you all right?" Faison asked as he held Ta'shauna in his arms. She shook her head no and sobbed into his silk shirt. He kissed the top of her head and rubbed her back, telling her that everything was going to be okay.

"I'm sorry, T, I'm sorry. I shouldn't have left you out there." He kissed the top of her head. "Please forgive me,

I'm                                    sorry,                                    okay?"

"It's okay, he woulda just killed us both." She looked up at him with vacant eyes, wetness bleeding down her face. "It's alright, I forgive you."

"I love you."

"I love you, too."

Faison's face twisted with anger as he held his sister in his arms, looking over all of the dead bodies of his goons and his family.

*Oh, it's on now, homeboy, I'ma 'bout to bring it to yo' ass, that's on my momma, bitch.*

\*\*\*

Faison sat at the dining room table with his leg out-stretched over a chair. His face winced in pain as the doctor dug into his leg with a medical instrument, pulling the metal slug from out of him and dropping it into a tin bowl. Once the doctor was done, he cleaned up Faison's wound, applied dressing and wrapped it with medical tape. He picked up the bowl and headed into the bathroom to cleanse everything.

When he returned, Faison was already popping the top on one of the two bottles of pain killers he had sitting on the dining room table. Faison washed the pills down with a sip from his glass of Cognac. He looked to the doctor and he had his hand out. Faison pulled a wad of money from his pocket, removed the gold money-clip and peeled off a few Benjamin Franklins, handing them to the doctor. Once the doctor finished counting the bills, he picked up his black leather medical bag and headed for the door.

"Just take my money and leave, huh? No, how you do-ing? How's the fiancé and kid, none of that shit, huh?" he called out to him.

"Hey, you don't pay me for my friendship," the good doctor replied. "You wanna knock down a couple of cold ones and shoot the shit then it's gonna cost ya."

"What?" Faison twisted his lips and gave him the side eye. "Man, get the fuck up from out here." He waved at him.

"That's what I thought." The doctor went on about his business.

As soon as the doctor disappeared through the doorway, Majestic, Smack and Don Juan were appearing through it. They filed inside of the dining room and sat around at the round table. Faison turned around to the table and clapped his hands. His butler emerged with an expensive bottle of Cognac on a golden platter along with a bucket of ice. He filled the glasses sitting before the guests with ice cubes and filled them with the dark liquor. Once he was done, he turned to Faison.

"That will be all, Higgins," Faison told the butler. The butler gave a nod and vanished through the doorway of the kitchen. Once the butler had gone, the chat amongst the men began.

"Young Blood, what happen out there today?" Majestic asked as he put fire to his black pipe and sucked on the end of it, causing smoke to waft.

"Yeah, man, what went down at the hospital?" Don Juan inquired as he picked up his glass of Cognac.

"I heard youngin' got active, laid quite a few folks down," Smack said, sipping from the glass of Cognac.

Faison nodded and said, "Yeah, my mother, my father, my uncle and two of my best men got hit out there."

"Say *what*?" Majestic said leaning closer along with Smack and Don Juan. What Faison said garnered all of their attention. "Are they all right?"

Faison shook his head no. "Everyone is dead," he said behind glassy bloodshot eyes. The first thing that came to mind was the senseless beef he had with his father. He wished he would have patched things up with his old man when he was alive, but now it was too late. He was gone and he wasn't ever coming back. *Damn!* If only this was a nightmare, but it wasn't. It was reality, his reality.

Faison was hurt, but he held his game face. He refused to show vulnerability to the men present. He couldn't allow them to see him as weak. Reputation was everything in the underworld. "I got shot tryna save my sister, barely escaped with my life. If it wasn't for the police and the ghetto bird coming, I would have been finished."

"Damn, nigga touching family." Majestic shook his head. "In my time a man's blood was off limits."

"This new breed of gangsta doesn't respect nothing, or nobody," Smack said. He looked to Don Juan and Faison. "No offense."

"None taken," Don Juan said. "It's not really the 80s babies though, it's these young niggaz from outta the 90s. Tiaz's is a wild card, so I'm willing to make an exception. Crim is off the chain." He took a sip of Cognac.

"This mothafucka has got to be eradicated." Smack spoke on it. "It's the only way we're gonna be able to walk out the house without having to look over our shoulders."

"I agree. We just gotta find this nuisance, slip a noose over his head and hang his black ass." Majestic gave a visual with both of his hands then balled his fists. His moment of rage came and went like the wind. He went back to smoking his black pipe, like he hadn't just blacked out a second ago.

"Like you said, we have to find him first." Don Juan scratched his goatee anxiously. He wanted Tiaz eliminated as soon as possible. He was somewhat fearful of the thug's ruthlessness. At any given time he could reappear and snatch up any one of them, and do whatever to them he damn well pleased. This didn't sit right with him and he wanted the brazen young hoodlum out of his hair.

"My son's mother used to fuck with'em." Faison told them all. This brought frowns to all of their faces. "Don't look at me like that. The only reason I didn't step to her was 'cause I didn't want her running to tell'em I was looking for'em and risk him going into hiding. I didn't tell y'all 'cause I didn't want chu mothafuckaz egging me to press her. I also didn't want to involve her. Y'all have wives and girlfriends, I'm sure you can understand where I'm coming from."

Everyone nodded their heads. They all came from a different world than their significant others and wanted to keep them out of their dealings in the streets. What they didn't know wouldn't hurt them, nor could it get any of the men indicted.

"If she doesn't fuck with homie any more, then what makes you think she knows where he is?" Don Juan inquired.

"You know how these females are, man, they're tender hearted." Faison told him. "They break up with a nigga one week and are back with'em the next. She may or may not know where he's laying low, but I can ask."

"Well, we need to holla at cha BM then." Don Juan sat back in his chair.

"I second that motion." Majestic sucked on the end of his black pipe. Smack fanned the smoke from out of his face with his hand. The nicotine irritated him.

"Yeah, Faison, you need to put a call in to your son's mother," Smack told him.

"Why call her when we can go see her?" Faison said.

Don Juan's cell phone rang and vibrated, stealing everyone in attendance attention. He pulled it out of his pocket and looked down at the screen. "Excuse me y'all, but I'ma have to take this. What's up with it?" He listened to what the caller was saying to him and a devilish grin formed on his lips. The fellas watched him attentively, wondering what was being discussed, some of them exchanging hushed whispers. Once he was done he disconnected the call and stood up.

"I'ma have to take a rain check," he stated.

This news brought forth exchanged whispers amongst the man. They weren't feeling him just getting up and leaving. One of them decided to speak up.

"Fuck you going, nigga?" Majestic's forehead creased with lines.

"I got business to attend to, pops. But once y'all sit that boy in a coffin, be sure to bang my line." He walked off, with a devious smirk on his face. He knew his associates were tight about him leaving, but he didn't give a shit though. He'd just gotten a call from a very reliable source that had given him Tiaz's address. He was all for tracking down the jack boy and making him pay for the sins he'd committed against him, but he wanted him all to himself. He wanted to be the soul that pushed his ass to an early death, and he was sure he wouldn't be able to do that with the fellas in on the plan.

*Nuh uh, he's all mine.*

Tranay Adams

# Chapter Fourteen

Chevy made her way up the steps of Savon's home. She lifted up the *welcome* mat and picked up the house key. She unlocked the door and stepped inside. A spear of light cut through the living room and dawned on the sofa. She stood in the doorway taking in the décor of the living room. There was a 70 inch Vizio flat screen, a black Italian leather sofa, white mink carpeted floors and a black wood coffee table with a glass top. Black and white portraits of entertainment figures lined the walls: The Rat Pack, Al Pacino, Robert Deniro, Sydney Portier, etc.

Chevy closed the door behind her and headed down the hall towards Savon's bedroom. She pushed her way inside and flipped on the lightswitch, opening the closet door. The light bulb that dangled from the ceiling came on when she pulled its drawstring, giving the space life. She got down on her knees and felt around on the floor of the closet, until she found what she was looking for, then peeled a flap of the carpet back and exposed a black iron digital safe. A tiny green bulb beeped and flashed after she entered the combination on the keypad, then the door popped open. Chevy pulled the door open and smiled at the Benjamin Franklins stored inside, then unzipped the Gucci duffle bag she'd brought along and opened it. She dipped her hand inside of the safe and removed the bands, one by one. By her estimation, the amount of money that was there with each band that she dropped into the duffle bag was close to $300,000 dollars. Once she'd cleaned the safe out, she closed the door and dropped the flap of carpet on it, making sure to smoothe the flap of carpet out so that it would blend it with the rest of the carpet surrounding it, before turning out the light and leaving the bedroom. Chevy unlocked the front door.

As soon as she stepped a foot out onto the porch, a gloved hand grabbed the lower half of her face and squeezed it tightly. Before Chevy could look to see who had grabbed her, she was being forced back into the house and slammed up against the wall. The grip of the gloved hand grew tight, so tight that she could hear the bone of her bottom jaw beginning to crack. The pressure surrounding her mouth was so strong that it brought tears to her eyes. She tried to speak, but the grip of the hand was too great. Air couldn't even flow through her mouth. She had to breathe as best as she could through her nose.

Chevy's heart was pounding behind her left breast. She was scared and didn't know what was about to occur. A pair of menacing eyes moved toward hers. The street lights shining through the slight openings of the blinds and into the living room, filled out some of the assailant's facial features. Although she could only distinguish parts of his face, his identity clearly registered inside of her head. He was Tiaz. He held a lone finger to his lips, signaling for her to be quiet. His gloved hand released its grip around her mouth and dipped below her chin, slipping its fingers around her throat and applying minimal pressure.

"I gotta situation on my hands," Tiaz began, eyes bleeding hatred as his hot breath moistened her face. "Me and your fiancé are beefing real hard right now. He killed Kantrell, Threat, and now he's looking to kill me. What I need from you is addresses of where he lays his head and places he frequents. Hell, I'll even take the address on a very close family member. Wait a minute, where's Te'Qui? He'll do." At the mention of her son's name, Chevy squirmed under his grip.

"No, leave Te'Qui alone he doesn't have anything to do with whatever is going on between you and Faison."

"True." He nodded. "But it's a dirty game and I gotta play it as such, if I want to win. Now you either tell me where lil' homie is, or the whereabouts of his punk ass daddy."

Chevy shook her head no as tears snaked down her face. "Fuck you!" she barked, raining spittle in his face. She harped up phlegm and spat it in his face. He closed his eyes as the goo oozed down along the side of his nose and over his lips then chuckled. His face contorted into a demonic expression and he produced a .44 magnum revolver right before her eyes. He pressed the cold steel against her forehead and she closed her eyes tight, waiting to hear the shot that would claim her life.

"What did you just say to me?" Chevy didn't answer this time. "Fuck you just say? Maybe you'll remember in the next life." He pulled the trigger of the revolver and it clicked empty, startling Chevy and causing her to sob loudly. She was terrified and didn't know what to do. She knew she wasn't going to lead Tiaz to her son. That was her baby boy and she'd die before she gave him up. And she sure wasn't going to give him Faison either. He was the boy's father and even though she'd been through the wringer with him, she knew that he still loved her and would always have her back. "That first chamber was empty, but rest assured this next one gon' leave Ragu plastered to the wall, so choose your response wisely. Okay, I'm gonna ask you again, where the fuck is Faison? You can either give him up or your boy. Doesn't really matter to me."

Chevy calmed down and gathered herself. She swallowed hard and said, "Go fuck yourself!" defiantly as she stared him dead in his eyes.

Pissed off, Tiaz went to pull the trigger and the front door was torn from its hinges by a powerful force. The door crashed onto the living room floor and three armed men walked upon it as they spilled inside. He placed Chevy in a chokehold, and walked her backwards into the kitchen. He stopped once he bumped up against the refrigerator. His head darted from left to right as the men closed in on him. His forehead wrinkled when he began to recognize who the threesome was. There was Faison who was walking with the assistance of a cane, Majestic, and Smack. Each man had a pistol of his own in his hand. Tiaz couldn't believe that all of his enemies were in one room with him. They were all mad dogging him, but he wasn't intimidated. Mean mugs didn't move him. Someone had to show him something. It wasn't like he hadn't been faced with three to one odds before. He'd been to prison, for Christ's sake. Every day he had a knucklehead or some crew trying to get at him. Tiaz placed his revolver to Chevy's temple, wishing a mothafucka would try him.

"Y'all niggaz back the fuck up, or on my momma she going to sleep forever!" he warned.

Faison, Majestic, and Smack stopped where they were. Majestic and Smack parted and a dark figure stepped from between them on forearm crutches. Tiaz's eyes narrowed into slits trying to see who it was. The dark figure stepped forth into what little light there was, smiling wickedly with a pistol in his hand.

"Long time no see," TJ said to Tiaz.

For a time he didn't say a word, he didn't recognize the man standing before him. But then his eyes wandered to the fading tattoo of a pit bull on his neck. Once he realized who the man in the forearm crutches was, he looked up into his cold dark eyes. "Tim Dog." Tiaz's face hardened and his top lip quivered with anger. Tim Dog was the same cat that robbed Ta'shauna and punched her in the eye. Tiaz had caught him slipping in a *Jack in the Box* parking lot and shot his legs up. Before he could finish him off the police came to his rescue.

"I could go a lifetime without seeing your ugly fucking face," Tiaz shot back.

His smart ass remark wiped the wicked smile right off of TJ's face. Angry, he slung the forearm crutch from his right arm and pointed his banger at Tiaz.

"Put the gun down or I'ma dome her!" Tiaz swore.

"I don't give a shit, she ain't my bitch!" TJ spat back.

"Nigga, are you crazy? That's my son's mother he's holding." Faison frowned.

"Exactly," TJ said. "She's *your* son's mother, not mine."

Faison pointed his banger at TJ's temple, resting his finger on the trigger. "Drop your goddamn gun, now!"

Hearing the metallic click of a hammer, Faison's eyes darted to his left. Majestic was pointing something shiny and chrome at the side of his face. "Now that may be the mother of your child, but that's my nephew. If I were you, I'd take that gun from his head."

Faison pulled a second banger from his waistline that was equipped with an extended magazine. He pointed it at Majestic's forehead. These niggaz had him all of the way fucked up if they just thought he was going to let his son's mother go out like that. He never stopped loving Chevy. He'd die for her and he'd kill for her. And it looked like he was going to have to prove it.

A flicker of movement at the corner of Faison's eye brought his attention over to Smack. He'd just drawn down on him.

"That's my friend of forty years you're pointing that there pistol at." Smack gave him a little history. "And I don't take kindly to it, son. I suggest you lower your piece."

Faison took his gun away from Majestic and brought it over to Smack.

"What the fuck is this?" Tiaz looked around at all of the men. He couldn't believe what just had unfolded before his eyes.

"Faison," Smack began, "this doesn't have to get ugly, son. Take your gun away from TJ's head and we'll lower ours. Our main focus is that bastard that has your son's mother hemmed up. We're here to get rid of him, we've united for this common goal. Don't lose sight of it."

"Him first." Faison nodded to TJ.

"I'm not lowering shit!" TJ spat. "This prick left me a cripple for the rest of my life! I'm willing to die to get a piece of his ass!" He gave Tiaz the evil eye and he gave it back.

"Don't be stupid, son!" Smack told him.

"Fuck that nigga!" Tim Dog barked back. "He can kiss my bony ass!"

"Harold, talk some sense into the boy, why don't you?" Smack said to Majestic.

"The time for talking has passed. It's time to take action." Majestic said calmly as he glared at Faison.

"What?" Smack's forehead wrinkled as he stared at his old friend with disbelief. He looked around at all of the men. All of them were wearing hard faces and were ready to get it popping. He was at the mercy of a Mexican standoff. "Fuck it then." He removed his fedora and threw it aside. "In the words of the late Marvin Gaye, let's get it on."

There was a moment of silence and then all hell broke loose. The living room came to life with flickers of light and gunshots. When the smoke cleared everyone was lying about on the floor, moaning and groaning in pain. Smack was dead, but Majestic, TJ and Faison were still alive.

Realizing that Tiaz was distracted with everything that had occurred, Chevy wanted to try to break loose from his grip and run, but the fear of catching a hot one in the back and ending up paralyzed slowed her roll.

Still holding Chevy in the chokehold, the buff neck thug surveyed the damage. Majestic and TJ were lying on their backs, holding their stomachs and grunting from their wounds. Faison was lying slumped against the wall, a bleeding hole in his chest and stomach. His facial expression was one of shock and excruciation. Tiaz shoved Chevy to the floor and ran out of the house.

She crawled toward Faison, sobbing. Tears rolled down her cheeks and splashed onto the hardwood floor as she moved forth on her hands and knees. She examined his wounds and the blood was soaking through his shirt.

The sight made her cringe.

Seeing Faison lying there bleeding like that with his life hanging in the balance made Chevy realize just how much she was still very much in love with him, despite all of their issues. He had always been there for her and their son. His love was a bitter, yet sweet one, but he breathed for his family.

Tiaz on the other hand was something different altogether. She knew then that her biggest mistake was hooking up with him. His presence had turned her world upside down. The short time that they were together caused more damage than her ex-fiancé's infidelity. She only wished she could turn back the hands of time, but sadly she couldn't. She had to deal with the consequences of her choices.

"You gon' be okay, alright? I'm gonna get chu to a hospital."

"I. I. Love you." He managed to say.

"I love you, too." Chevy told him as she caressed his forehead and kissed it. He tried to say something else. "Shhh, don't try to talk, baby." Hearing the moans and groans of Majestic and TJ, snapped her head in their direction. She picked up Faison's gun and approached the injured men in their agony. She wore the mask of a derange killer as she deposited two into Majestic's chest, putting him out of his misery. She stepped to TJ, who was holding his bleeding stomach and spewing blood from his mouth. His eyes zeroed in on the banger in her hand and then to her tear slicked face. Realizing what she had intended to do, he mad dogged her.

"Go ahead and do you, bitch!" he shouted. "All the hell I done been through, heaven is gon' welcome me with open arms! Shoot me! Shoot me, bitch!"

*Bloc! Bloc! Bloc! Bloc! Bloc! Bloc!*

Police sirens wailed from afar as Chevy stared down at TJ. She watched as he stared passed her and gave his last breath. She then stuffed the murder weapon into the Gucci duffle bag, zipped it up and slung it over her shoulder.

"Come on, baby." She grabbed Faison's hand in an attempt to pull him up to his feet.

"Arghhh!" His eyes narrowed as he clenched his jaws, feeling jolts of pain shoot through his body, trying to get up. "I can't. I can't. Leave me. Leave me be."

"I'm not leaving you, you've gotta get up!"

"I can't. Go on."

"No, goddamn it! You came this far, you don't get to lay down and die now!" she spoke sharply. "The Thompson Cousins, jail, the indictments, the countless murder attempts. I didn't get engaged to no weak ass man, sweetheart. A soldier put a ring on my finger. A soldier, you hear me, Faison? A soldier!" She pulled on his arm as he struggled to get up. "Now on your feet, Reed, get on your goddamn feet!"

"Arrrr!" He came up, nearly falling on top of her, but she held fast, holding him in her embrace.

"Haa! Haa! Haa!" She panted out of breath, winded having to help pull him up. "It's alright, it's okay. I got chu, I got chu, you hear me?"

"Yeahhh." He gritted from the pain.

"Come on, let's go." She threw his arm over her shoulders. They made their way out of the back door of the house, just as the police made it onto the scene.

\*\*\*

Tiaz slid into his car and resurrected it, pulling away from Savon's house as police sirens filled the air.

He continuously looked over his shoulder as he sped away, adrenalin pumping and heart thumping. He couldn't believe things played out the way that they did back at the house. He was expecting to shake up Chevy when he followed her from home to gather some intelligence on Faison, but shit took a turn for the worse. He wasn't worried about it though. Three of his enemies were gone which left one on his hands to deal with. *Don Juan!*

Tranay Adams

# Chapter Fifteen
## *Meanwhile on the other side of the city*

Te'Qui hated himself for not being able to save Baby Wicked from his demise. He was looking for the Nissan Pathfinder to roll up, not a gold Celebrity. By the time it registered in his head what was going down, the MP-5 had already rattled off. He'd drawn his banger, but it was too late. Maniac had already laid Baby Wicked down on the corner and the Celebrity was speeding away from the scene. Te'Qui felt like he had let his best friend down. He was counting on him to hold him down, but he failed. His slip up cost his right hand his life and he was solely to blame. He felt the hurt inside of him, stirring his emotions and urging him to let go and let the tears fall. Although his heart begged for him to grieve, he wouldn't oblige. He remembered what his friend had said to him before he was killed.

*"Anything can happen in this game we're playing, so if my enemies steal me from this world, don't cry for me, ride for me, homie, straight up."*

Te'Qui didn't expect either of them to die so soon. They were both young and had their lives ahead of them. He realized then that the life was no joke. It was a monster that gobbled down everyone it came across: young, old, innocent, ignorant, smart. Whoever was in its path got eaten.

Te'Qui sat at the edge of his bed in deep thought. The sound of a honking horn snapped him back to reality and drew his attention to his bedroom window. He pulled the curtain back and peered through the window. A turquoise green Ford Taurus sat idling at the curb in front of his house. He let the curtain fall back over the window and pulled open his dresser drawer, reached under the folded boxers inside and removed the .38 special. The pistol he stashed in the pocket of his California Republic hoodie, threw his hood over his head and headed out of the door.

He sprinted across the lawn and hopped into the front passenger seat of the Taurus. As soon as his ass graced the peanut butter leather seat, Wicked pulled off. He was dressed in a black stocking cap and sweatshirt. His hands were covered by black Nike baseball gloves. He piloted the vehicle with one hand, while he took swigs from a flask. He hissed as the dark liquor bit his throat then passed the flask to Te'Qui. The young nigga took a swig and his face twisted as the strong alcohol engulfed his esophagus like a bath of flames. He wiped his mouth with a gloved hand and passed the flask back. Once Wicked screwed the cap back on the flask, he slipped it into the pocket of his black Dickies. The ride to their destination was quiet as both of them were in their own thoughts, preparing themselves mentally for the mission at hand.

Tonight was the night that Te'Qui was to lay down the cats that had robbed him of his ace. His heart was beating out of control and he was nervous as shit. He'd shot a gun before, but never at someone with intentions to kill. The only thing he had murked was motionless, lifeless objects, which was a far cry from a living and breathing human being.

His mental was bombarded with images of Baby Wicked being shot down on the corner that night. All he could see were the faces of agony his friend made as the small fires in his frame burned and plasma oozed from out of him and onto the sidewalk. The thought of his friend experiencing such excruciating pain made his face morph into a mask of hatred. He clenched his teeth and the skeletal bone structure of his jaws emerged. He found himself sneering thinking about how he had been done up. Unconsciously, his hand gripped the pistol in the pocket of his hoodie.

A tap on his chest awoke him from his thoughts. He looked over to Wicked and he nodded at the windshield. Through the windshield he saw a white Dodge Charger pull into a Shell gas station, pumping Nipsey Hussle's *Killa* loud as a mothafucka. The Charger rolled up to an air & water machine. The driver side door opened and Time Bomb hopped out. He checked the air in his front tire then proceeded over to the machine where he deposited two quarters into the machine and grabbed the air nozzle, bobbing his head to the music pulsating from his ride. He was in his own world, ignorant of the impending danger that was amidst he and his homeboy.

"That's Time Bomb that's about to put the air into the tire," Wicked told him, "that nigga, Maniac, is in the passenger seat, he's the one that slumped baby bro, right?" Te'Qui nodded yes. "I got him, Time Bomb is yours."

Te'Qui wanted Maniac for himself since he was the one that actually killed Baby Wicked. But he understood that he'd have to fall back and let big brother get at him. Although Te'Qui and Baby Wicked were tight and as good as brothers, Wicked and his brother were family and blood ties ran deep. So it was Wicked's right to want to claim vengeance in the name of his sibling.

Te'Qui nodded and said, "Alright." While he was checking the chamber of his revolver, Wicked was pulling a black .9mm automatic from underneath his seat. He chambered a round into the head of the weapon and laid it down in his lap. He slowly pulled into the gas station and crept up on Time Bomb. When the Crip looked up and saw the Taurus without the headlights trying to creep on him, he dropped the air nozzle and made a run for it. Wicked floored the gas pedal and hit him, causing him to flip over the windshield and crash to the ground. Wicked and Te'Qui hopped out of the

Taurus like a couple of troops on Iraq soil on a mission. Red bandana covering the lower halves of their faces, head bussas in their grips. It was on now.

Maniac's door swung open and he came up holding a Tec-9, face twisted in hatred, teeth gritted. The holey barrel of his weapon flared and spat fire in Wicked's direction. He dipped below the spitting barrel and aimed his banger at Maniac's torso through the driver side window. He cracked off four rounds, each shot splattered blood out of Maniac's back and caused him to stagger backwards and fall to the ground. He ran upon him as he was hollering out in agony and clutching at his wounded frame. When Wicked's shadow eclipsed him, he grew quiet and his eyes shifted up to him. He scowled angrily and spewed profanities his way.

"This is from my brother, through me, straight to you!" Wicked spat with venom in his tone before handing down the Death Sentence in the form of four rounds to Maniac's face. He kicked his kill's corpse for good measure before walking over to his accomplice. He witnessed the youngster shoot Time Bomb's legs out from under him as he tried to crawl away. When he fell on his stomach, he kicked him in his ribs, forcing him to turn over onto his back. The Crip grimaced as he stared up at his would be executioner. A light bulb of recognition came on inside of his head and he wished Maniac had killed him along with his friend that night.

Wicked came to stand beside Te'Qui as he pointed his banger at Time Bomb's chest.

"Gon' and twist that nigga, Blood, so we can get outta here." He urged him.

Te'Qui wore a hard face as he looked his prey dead in his eyes. Again his mental was assaulted with images of Baby Wicked in agony as he lay dying that night. The images lit a dynamite of hatred inside of him and it exploded. Finally here was the time, finally here was the place. This bitch ass nigga was about to get his and his best friend could finally rest in peace.

*Bop! Bop! Bop! Bop!*

Four hot ones penetrated Time Bomb's chest, killing him instantly. Te'Qui took the time to admire his handiwork before hopping back into the Taurus with Wicked and fleeing the murder scene.

*** 

Uche and Uduka hopped off of the bus and made their way down 77th and Figueroa. They received the occasional glance and barks from neighboring dogs. However, they didn't pay them any mind, they were focused on their destination. The house they were looking for was coming up just on the right hand side. It was a brown and tan colored home with a rusting fence and a dirt patched lawn. Its porch was dark, but they could see the embers and the exhausting of smoke, as well as the shadows moving. There was laughter and chit chat that the brothers couldn't quite make out, but when they'd drawn closer, the noise settled and they heard a man's voice.

"Yo, who are these mothafuckaz, man?" one voice said.

"I don't know, but if they tryna creep, they're in for a rude awakening."

*Click Clack! Click Clack! Clack! Rack! Pact!*

The familiar sounds of guns being cocked did nothing to cause the siblings to proceed with caution. Shit, there wasn't anything that they feared. The horrors that they experienced in their lifetime had branded some of the most gruesome images into their brains and had prepared them for all of the ugly that this cold, cruel world had to offer. Uche pushed open the gate and entered the yard with Uduka on his heels. They hadn't gotten half way up the path before a couple of hardheads emerged from the shadows of the porch, each one gripping a gun of his own.

"Fuck is y'all niggaz?" A young nigga rocking a stocking cap asked.

"Where y'all from?" Another in a black Dickie suit questioned. Seeing the hard faces and guns set off an alarm in Uche's head. He tilted his head downward and stared up at the competition with a tight jaw. His hand slipped inside of his suit's jacket. His fingers curled around the spear he'd stashed there. He was about to draw it and attack until his brother grabbed his arm and gave him a look.

Uduka looked from his brother to the hostiles. "We are from Nigeria," he started off. "I am Uduka and dis is ma brudda, Uche. We are da bruddas of Boxy." He looked around at all of the faces of the men, hoping that the uttering of his brother's name would put them at ease being that he was from their neighborhood, but it didn't. They remained as they were when the brothers first arrived, hostile. They all knew Boxy and had some sort of relationship or dealings with him, but neither of them had laid eyes on the foreigners.

"Who y'all looking for?" Stocking cap asked.

"We've come to see Gatz," Uduka answered.

"Well, the homies don't know y'all or trust y'all," he said. "So we're not gone show y'all to Gatz, we gone show y'all spear chucking asses to God."

When the hostiles went to point their guns, the brothers drew their spears and stood side by side, fearlessly. They knew they didn't have a snowball's chance in hell against the rain of bullets that were to come, but they dropped their nuts anyway. Their father, Timon, taught them to embrace death like they did life, because one day it was sure to come. These were his last words before being shot down defending their village from marauders.

"Hold up!" A voice rang from the porch, halting everyone's next move. The men stood still with their weapons pointed at the Nigerians, while they stood frozen, their eyes darting around at everyone.

After the voice, a man came rolling down the ramp of the porch in a wheelchair. He was sporting a doorag with the flap and mustard gold Jamaican tank top with a couple of thin gold necklaces. A toothpick fidgeted at the corner of his mouth as his black leather weight lifting gloved hands rolled his chair toward the foreigners, causing his homeboys to part like the Red Sea.

His head moved from left to right studying the brothers' faces. He relaxed when he recalled who they were.

Uche and Uduka relaxed a bit seeing that it was Gatz, but they were still on guard for the impending drama.

"They good, y'all." He held up his gloved hand and his homeboys lowered their guns. "Y'all remember me?" he asked the siblings. The brothers had been to America once before to visit Boxy. During that time, they'd met Gatz at his home where he was throwing a barbeque for one of the homies who'd been released from prison. They chopped it up for a time and got to know a little bit about each another.

The brothers gave a slight nod. "Sorry about cha people. Boxy was a pain in the ass to most, but he was alright by me. Hell, he brought me this chair." *Ting! Ting! Ting!* He tapped the arm-rest of his transportation with the gold wedding band on his finger. The wheelchair was sitting up all pretty and shit, dripped in chrome with rims. It had side view mirrors like the ones on a motorcycle and a comfy black leather seat and back rest. This was the Cadillac of wheelchairs. Boxy had copped it for Gatz on the account of him getting shot in the spine when he rode on some Mexicans that had took him for some crack in a robbery that left him with one in the shoulder and two of their homeboys dead.

"What can I do for y'all?" Gatz asked, by this time they'd stashed their spears in their hiding places.

"We need," Uduka looked around and leaned closer, "protection."

"You niggaz got money?" he asked like *'cause ain't shit free.*

Uduka nudged Uche and he reached inside of his suit's jacket, pulling out a wad of wrinkled Dead Presidents secured by a beige rubberband. When Gatz saw the money, a broad smile procured his gruffly face.

"Shops open then." He spread his arms welcomingly. He spun around in his wheelchair, waving for the siblings to follow him as he rolled down the driveway.

Gatz opened the garage door and rolled inside. He flipped on the light switch and gave birth to the items stored. There was an array of shit. It looked like a junkyard, but this was just a cover up since this acted as a home base for the illegal operation he was running.

"Close that door behind you, Duke." Gatz spun around in the wheelchair, parking beside a refrigerator that looked like it had seen better days. He motioned the brothers over and they fell in step. He opened the refrigerator and removed the door panel. Inside there were handguns ranging from different shapes, sizes, and calibers, residing on hooks. "Brand new, just for you," he sung. He took the toothpick from his mouth and leaned down, pulling open the drawers. There were bullets, shotgun shells, and magazines stored. When he came back up, he opened the freezer door and exposed a variety of shotguns and assault rifles. He rolled back in his chair a little and motioned his customers over so that they could take a look at all his store had to offer.

Uche and Uduka picked up different guns, examining them and checking to see how many rounds they held. They ended up settling on .45 automatic handguns. Growing up, their uncle had taught them how to shoot, but they preferred knives to guns. They believed that guns were for cowards, seeing as how their unarmed father had been killed by one protecting their home.

Uche held tight to the black .45, while Uduka adopted the chrome one with the ivory handle. They grabbed a couple of magazines and boxes of shells, paid Gatz for his merchandise, dapped him up, and left.

"Aye," Gatz called Uche back. He turned around holding the garage door open. "Y'all need anything else, you be sure to come back now, ya hear?" The oldest of the Eme Brothers nodded and continued out of the garage, leaving the gun merchant counting up the money he'd made. Heading out of the garage, they passed a bronze skinned kid in a Houston fitted cap and Chicago Bears hoodie, rocking heavy gold jewels over it. He threw his head back slightly like *what's up?* and went on about his business which was inside of the garage.

"What's up my nigga, Gatz?" They heard the kid say. "Them nines came in yet?"

"Yeah, yeah, yeah, I gotchu faded," Gatz said back. "But close the door though, Juvie. I don't need the whole hood in mine."

"My fault, hold up." There was squeaking as the garage door was closed.

Uche and Uduka continued on their way. Now that they had guns, it was time that they found the people they needed to use them on. They weren't sure where to start their search first, but when they did come upon their brother's killer, they weren't going to open their mouths. They were going to let their guns do all of the talking.

*\*\**

Wicked killed the headlights of the Ford Taurus and made a right, coasting down a path between two warehouses that had been shut down some time ago. After bodying the engine, he looked over his shoulder where he saw a cherry red BMW 750 awaiting. A smirk curled the corner of his lips and he turned back around, retrieving the Slim Jim where it rested beside his leg on the floor. He popped the trunk by pushing a button just below the dashboard. *Thunk!* He nudged Te'Qui and they hopped out of the car, making their way to its rear. He tucked the Slim Jim at the small of his back and pulled out two gas cans, passing one to his accomplice. Together, they soaked the stolen vehicle. Its dashboard, its seats, its floors, even its outside was doused with the flammable liquid.

"Go get in the car." Wicked threw his head toward the BMW.

"Who's in there?" Te'Qui inquired.

"A friend," he simply replied. Once he saw him jogging toward the getaway ride, he poured a line of gasoline that led about ten feet from the Taurus before slinging the gas can aside. Pulling out a book of matches, he snatched a stick free and swiped it across the black strip at the back of it. The head of the match glowed red like heated charcoal and emitted smoke. He admired its burning for a spell before tossing it on the line of gas. *Frooosh!* A line of fire zipped up the path en route to the Taurus. He turned his back, pulling off his gloves and tucking them into his right back pocket. He strolled off casually, like he was just heading to the super market to pick up a carton of milk for a bowl of cereal.

\*\*\*

Te'Qui's running slowed to a jog as he neared the BWM. He made out a pair of wrinkly hands and a floral dress. The fragrance he inhaled was rich and strong. Sort of like the perfume he used to smell on the older women his Aunt Gretchen played Spades with. The scent was very familiar though. He'd come across it several times before. It belonged to only one woman he could think of and he couldn't believe his eyes when he saw her sitting behind the wheel.

"Ms. Helen?" His brows crinkled as he closed the door to the backseat shut. He was taken aback when he feasted his youthful eyes upon her. He expected one of Wicked's girls, one of his homeboys even, but not his aunt. *What the hell is she doing here?* he thought. Reasons ran through his head like a Giselle on the run from its predator. At the moment she'd just finished burning a cigarette down to its butt and flicked it out of the window. She didn't pay him any mind as she picked up her can of beer and took it to the head.

Normally, Te'Qui would have found this odd, because she was always pleasant when he came over to her house to visit Baby Wicked, but he was too jacked up off of his adrenaline from the events of the evening to notice her sudden change in attitude.

Aunt Helen took a swallow of beer and sat the can back down, turning her yellowing glassy eyes out of the front passenger side window. Te'Qui followed her line of vision and found Wicked at the end of it. He'd just set the fire and was in stride in their direction, tucking his gloves into his back pocket.

The fire he'd created engulfed their getaway car and lit the background behind him in a golden orange bed of flames. There was a flash of light and then an explosion, but he didn't even flinch. He was still in step like he didn't just see or feel that shit. He appeared to be moving in slow motion to Te'Qui. He looked mad, too. Not upset, but like he'd gone bat shit crazy. The faraway look in his eyes, coupled with the black rings under them, and the menacing smile didn't do much to help him either.

Wicked hopped into the front passenger seat and slammed the door shut. As soon as his Aunt Helen pulled off, the Taurus exploded for a second time. This time louder and with a greater light. On their way back to the house they could hear the fire trucks racing to the location they'd just left.

"You did real good tonight, my young nigga, real good." Wicked said to Te'Qui as he fished out a couple of items from the brown paper bag sitting between his sneakers. He withdrew two clear plastic cups and a Ziploc bag of ice. He dropped ice cubes into each one of the cups and poured them up with Coke and Hennessy, then sat the bottle of Hennessy down on the floor and passed the little nigga one of the cups. Taking casual sips of his drink, he watched Te'Qui indulge in the alcohol beverage through the sun-visor mirror. The youngster's eyes narrowed and his nose scrunched. He turned his head away from the cup and clutched his neck, feeling the hot liquid pour down his esophagus. He hissed and coughed, holding a fist to his mouth. No matter how many times he drank alcohol he could never get used to it. He really hated it. The only reason he even drank it was so he wouldn't look lame in front of the homies.

Seeing Te'Qui gagging and coughing, Wicked reached into the backseat and patted him on his back.

"I don't know what I was tripping on. I should have known yo' lil' ass couldn't drink with me." He cracked a smirk, which made him look creepy with the black rings under his eyes. "You straight?"

"Yeahhh." Te'Qui doubled over coughing and nodding. He sat back erect and took another sip of Hennessy. This time, he was taking it like he was born to do so.

"Yo', so how you feel since we done laid them bustas down that smoked baby bro?" Wicked inquired.

"Man, fuck them niggaz, Blood," he answered. "They got what was coming to them. I wish I could bring they asses back to life, just so I could smoke them again." He said with a hard face, sounding as hard as his heart had become.

"Sho' ya right." Wicked nodded. "But listen though. We took care of them pussies, but there's one more nigga's program we need to get with ASAP. You feel me?"

"Say no more, big homie," Te'Qui responded. "Just gimmie that thang and point me in his direction."

"That's what I'm talking about. We gotta soldier from the gang, swoowoop." He grinned approvingly. "Check it, I think you can gimme a lil' info on this fool I'm after."

Te'Qui frowned and his neck coiled.

"How you figure?"

"It's the cock sucker that gave y'all that shit to slang out there." He told him. "The way I see it, baby bro's blood is just as much on his hands as them crabs that murked him. See what I'm saying?" Te'Qui was taken aback by what he was just told. He looked away, thinking on it as he stared at the floor. He then turned his eyes back on Baby Wicked's brother.

"I can't tell you who gave us that work, Wicked. I promised him that I wouldn't," he admitted. He felt conflicted, being that Tiaz had whopped his mother's ass and almost killed her, but he had to still adhere to the code of the streets. Baby Wicked had drilled in his head to never snitch under any circumstances, so his lips were sealed. "I gave homeboy my word. Now I may not fuck with him like that no more, but my word is bond. I'ma stand up nigga, I'm sure you understand."

When he said this, Helen narrowed her eyelids and took a gander at him through the rearview mirror. She wasn't feeling him not cooperating. In fact, it pissed her off. She went to say something, but her nephew grabbed her hand. He locked eyes with her and shook his head no.

Wicked nodded as he swallowed the last of the liquor in his cup. He sat the cup aside and plucked a blunt from the ashtray. He held it pinched between his fingers as he fired it up, watching the tip of it burn and turn into an ember. He stashed the lighter back into his pocket and was about to take a hit when he looked to Te'Qui.

"You know what, my nigga, you popped your cherry tonight. You got down for yo' homeboy." He told him. "This here is a celebration. It's only right that the guest of honor gets the first few tokes." He passed him the blunt and he took it.

The youngster was relieved the air in the car had shifted and he thought Wicked was about to flip the fuck out. He was a bit surprised, seeing as how he dropped the subject just like that. But then again, getting his hands on the nigga that had given him and his brother the drugs should be minute, considering they'd already laid down the fools responsible for his death.

Te'Qui took the blunt with one hand and passed it to the other. Holding it pinched between his fingers, he took a couple of healthy draws, allowing the potent weed to fill his lungs. That shit was fiyah, real fiyah. He was starting to feel its affect already and he'd just hit it.

"Damn, Blood, where you get this from?" He looked up front to Wicked.

"Ahh, just a lil' something, something the homies blessed me with when I came home," he said like it wasn't a big deal. When little homie tried to pass him the blunt back he waved him off. "Nah, gon' ahead, that's all you." He massaged his chin and watched him attentively through the sun-visor mirror.

"So what chu thinking about naming me, Blood?"

"Q-ball."

"Q-ball?"

"Yeah." He nodded. "What? You don't like it?"

"Shit, if you like it, I love it."

A while after smoking, Te'Qui began to feel lightheaded. His brows furrowed and he looked to Wicked, seeing double. The twin images of him divorced and reunited three times. The youngster's eyes became hooded and his neck moved wobbly. He looked at the L pinched between his fingers and realized that he may have been poisoned. His forehead wrinkled and he looked to Wicked. "What the. What the fuck did you put in here?"

"Something that will put chu on yo' ass for a time, Blood." Wicked spoke, sounding like his voice had been chopped and screwed, like those songs from Houston produced by DJ Screw.

Wicked was a firm believer of not snitching, but when his little brother got peeled, all of that shit went out of the window. He wanted the mothafucka that gave his people that crack, bad. And he wasn't above torturing his younger sibling's best friend to do it. The way he saw it, if the little nigga was holding back information on a second party involved then his ass was just as guilty as him.

"Mothafucka…" Te'Qui dropped the L on the floor and watched its ember die. His eyes moved around lazily in his head as he tried to fight off the drug induced sleep, but eventually fell victim, heading into a world of darkness.

# Chapter Sixteen

It was hell trying to hail a cab back to the motel, so Uche and Uduka got directions on how to catch the bus back where they resided from an old wino begging for change to get a drink. Uduka stood behind his brother as he paid for both of their fares. He took in the full scope of the interior and saw that it crowded. There wasn't a place to sit so they'd definitely have to stand up on their ride back home. They made their way through the maze of bodies, taking in the stuffy air and the smells of the riders, some rancid, others not so much. They took up space near the rear of the bus, where they held onto their respective posts. At their back were two youngsters, looking to be between sixteen and eighteen years old. One was going on and on about something, while the other seemed to be listening intently. The Nigerians weren't paying them any mind, until their brother's name came up.

"Yeah, man, they took the boy, Boxy, in the back of the deli and did him up something nasty."One of the boys reported. "They said that nigga Don Juan took a machete," he gripped an imaginary machete with both hands, "and brought that bitch down into his head." He swung the imaginary machete downward.

Uche and Uduka gasped and exchanged glances, hearing the gruesome details of their brother's murder. Uduka made to let go of the post and approach the young men, but his brother grabbed his arm, stopping him.

"Wat? We can make 'em tell us where to find dis Don Juan." He whispered, frowning.

"We get 'em to talk and den dey run off to tell 'em we're looking for 'em."

Uduka settled down, realizing that his brother was right. They continued to listen to the young men's gossiping.

"Fuck outta here!" The other boy looked shocked. His eyes were bugged and his mouth was hanging open.

"Real spit."

"Nigga, how you know?" He gave him a disbelieving expression, with a side eye and twisted lips.

"You know them niggaz Juvie and Lil' Stan are like this." He hooked his fingers around one another. "I fuck with Stan's younger sister, April. She's the one that told me."

"Daaaamn, that nigga, Don, ain't playing out here. Dude like the black Tony Montana and shit."

"Yo,' this our stop." The boy that had been telling the story nudged his homeboy.

There was a sound like air was decompressing and then the bus came to a stop. The youngsters, along with several other passengers, moved to unboard.

Uche and Uduka locked eyes, their eyes narrowed and their jaws tightened. They knew exactly who they needed to find in order to apprehend their brother's murderer.

\*\*\*

The night was dark and cold as a loan shark's heart. The homies were all kicking it outside of Gatz' house, getting loaded and shit, kicking it about hood politics and reminiscing about Boxy. Their loud noise had brought along the cops, thanks to a complaining neighbor, but threats of violence shut them down from calling in any further infractions.

"My nigga is fuuuuuucked up." One of the homies made this acknowledgement. There were four of them, including him and Gatz. They were all kicking it outside of his yard sipping on clear plastic cups of brown liquor and blowing down blunts, as if they had an unlimited supply. Everyone was faded as a mothafucka and barely able to stand. Hell,

Gatz had even pissed himself twice that night, he was so far gone on the sauce.

The homies laughed and pointed as they watched the gun merchant's head move about like one of those boggle head dolls. His eyes were closed and he was snoring with drool streaming out the corner of his mouth, soiling his gray sweatshirt. He farted and his nose twitched.

"Gatz! Gatz!" Another one of the homies called out to him from where he was standing on the curb, plastic cup in hand observing him, amusingly.

A third homie smacked the wheelchair bound man across the cheek several times until he sprung to life. Swinging his left and then his right, his face twisted in anger. He was ready to knock a nigga on his ass. When this happened, the homie with the plastic cup leaned over the Navigator laughing and smacking its hood with his palm. Another one doubled over busting up, while the last fell to the sidewalk holding his stomach, cackling.

Relief overcame Gatz's face and he dropped his arms to his sides, cracking a smirk and shaking his head at his homeboys. They were all a bunch of clowns to him. They were all in their mid-thirties, but behaved like they were still in high school. The moment that they were living was like old times. He loved it.

It was sort of how it was back in the day when they would chill at the older homie, Termite's house, getting shit faced and shooting the breeze. Termite's crib was like the set's headquarters. They had meetings, parties, card games, dice games and even baby showers at his spot. Hell, it was there that Gatz had gotten put on the set. Right there in the homies backyard. He'd never forget the day. It was like the date of his birthday.

Sometimes Gatz regretted being paralyzed, being that he couldn't move around in the streets like the rest of the homies like he wanted to, but times like this definitely got his mind off of it.

The homie with the plastic cup downed the last of his liquor and tossed the cup aside. He belched and stretched his arms.

"Yo' man, we're about to shoot up to Starz, you tryna roll out or what?" he asked Gatz, inquiring if he wanted to hit the local strip club.

"Nah, I'm good." He looked himself over. "I gotta take a shower anyway. Messing around with y'all niggaz, I done pissed on myself like a goddamn baby."

"We'll wait while you get cleaned up."

"I'm straight," he replied. "I'ma shower and hit the sack. Probably get caught up on *Orange is the New Black* on Netflix."

"Alright then." The homeboys slapped hands with him and dipped off to the Navigator. The doors closed one after another and the enormous black truck resurrected. West Side Connection's *Let It Rain* came exploding from its confines, setting off the alarms to nearby parked cars.

*It ain't my fault you wanna C-walk*
*and gang bang when you hear the G-talk*
*Nigga swing that bitch 'til you break the ball joints*
*Niggas can't see me on this mic or this ballpoint*
*Papa Don got it locked (got it locked)*
*with the Glock got ya butt naked to ya socks yayae*
*The Westside Connect Thugs...Ain't no California Love just*
*California slugs*

The homie behind the wheel adjusted the sideview mirror, chucked up his hood at Gatz and he threw it back. He pulled off, but slammed on the brakes, nearly hitting the car in front of him. He backed up and slammed into the car behind him. *Shit*, he hissed, then threw the beast into drive and drove off, busting a U-turn in the middle of the residential block and speeding off. Drunk as a sailor, he swerved around from side to side. Gatz watched the Navigator with an amused expression until it bent the corner, out of sight. He then swung his wheelchair around and rolled into the yard, up the ramp and onto the front door of his house.

Pulling out his keys, he could have sworn he heard something on the other side. He turned his ear to the door and listened closely with a frown. When he didn't hear anything, he shrugged it off and opened the door. In the doorway the only thing that could be seen was his silhouette and the backdrop that was the bluish black sky with its moonlighting. He closed the door behind him and flipped on the lightswitch, becoming startled when he saw Uche sitting on his couch as if he paid rent in the mothafucka.

"What the..." Gatz scowled and bit down at the corner of his bottom lip. He didn't know why the Africans were inside of his crib, nor did he give a fuck. They fucked up the moment they entered his home without being permitted. He threw the blanket from over his legs and snatched up an automatic shotgun, racking it and pointing it at the foreigner. Uche's eyes slightly shifted upwards, alerting the gun merchant to someone else's presence. He went to swing the shotgun around and a telephone cord looped around his head, closing around his neck tightly. Before he knew it, he was flipping over in his chair, and trying to slip his fingers beneath the cord to stop from being strangled to death. His eyes turned glassy. He clenched his teeth and veins formed at his temples. Uduka's face was pulled tight at the center and his bottom lip was tucked into his mouth. Although he was pulling with all his might, he wasn't trying to kill him though. Nah, he was trying to make this mothafucka pass out.

"Gaggggahhhhh!" Gatz eyes rolled up into the back of his head and his tongue hung out of his mouth. His movements grew slower and slower, until he eventually met with darkness.

### Twenty minutes later

Gatz eyes flickered open and looked around. He realized his mouth was gagged and he was tied down to an old rusting table. Uduka stood beside him with an electric saw, while his brother stood off in the corner toying with the dial of a raggedy radio, trying to find a station. He stopped on Power 105.9. Biggie Smalls *You're Nobody 'Til Somebody Kills You* came roaring from the speakers.

"Ahhh, perfect." Uche said after finding the song. He stood tall.

"Yes, perfect, brudda." Uduka locked eyes with the gun merchant. The look in the young African's eyes made him nervous. From what Boxy had told him, the youngest of his brothers was the most innocent, but what he was seeing before him contradicted all of that. The kid standing beside him bore the face of a man possessed by satanic thoughts that he was dying to act upon. His eyes had a faraway look and he licked the lips of his sweaty face. The garage was hot as hell.

Gatz struggled to get loose from his restraints, but there wasn't any use because those ropes held his ass in place. He wasn't going anywhere unless the brothers wanted him to. Having grown tired, he settled and watched as the youngest of the Eme brothers sat the saw down on the rusting table and slipped off his suit's jacket, throwing it across the raggedy forest green sofa. He then smacked his hands together and stepped back to the table, looking his hostage up and down. He picked up the electric tool and squeezed the trigger, activating the blade. It spun rapidly, causing an eerie sound to fill the garage.

The gun merchant's head snapped to the left as he was trying to avoid the danger of the saw. Uduka seemed to be getting a kick out of watching him squirm under the threat of the power tool. Suddenly, he released the trigger and held the saw at his side.

"Tell us where Juvie is and we'll let cha live. Ya don't and ya die!"

"Fuck you! Fuck you!" Gatz spat muffled by the gag, scowling.

"Okay, muddafucka!" Uduka's face morphed into something horrific. He snatched up the electric saw. Squeezing the trigger, he rounded the table slicing his hostage's body, drawing muffled screams from him. The man's eyes became red webbed and rolled with tears. His shirt and jeans quickly absorbed his burgundy blood. Uduka swung the blade away, looking over his handiwork proudly.

"Ya ready ta talk now, Mistah Get Bad?" He breathed heavily, his hands and the tool speckled with blood.

"Fuck, fuck you!" he barked back muffled, tears pooling his eyes.

"Right." His eyes met his arms and an idea formed. "I find ya amusin' without legs, but wit out arms I'm sure ya will be more interestin.'"

Gatz's eyes snapped open and terror choked him about the neck. Seeing this made the younger Eme brother smiled wickedly. He started the power saw back up and brought it near the cripple's arm. He screamed to the top of his lungs. "Alright, okay! I'll tell you!"

Gatz gave him Juvie's whereabouts and Uche scribbled it down.

"Let's get outta here." Uduka picked up his jacket.

"Not so fast, finish 'em."

"What?"

"Keel 'em," he said it slower.

Uduka made a serious face and nodded. He passed his brother his jacket and approached the table, causing the weapon's dealer to scream and pled for his life. He pinched his nose closed and held a hand over his mouth. He watched as he struggled, eyes growing cocked before releasing his last breath.

"Satisfied?" he asked, slipping on his jacket.

"Very." He grabbed him about the neck and kissed the side of his head.

It was time to pay Juvie a visit.

***

Te'Qui came to blinking his eyes as if there was a bright light shining into them. Narrowing his eyelids, he looked about and discovered that he was inside of a decrepit basement. He looked himself over and saw that he was only clad in his Fruit of a Loom briefs. Hearing footsteps from above, he pushed off of the cold filthy floor and looked up at the ceiling. He listened to the footfalls and saw the debris falling, causing him to blink and rub his eyes.

He heard the basement door being unlocked and then swinging open. Then there were two pairs of feet as they made their way down the squeaky staircase. He kept his eyes on the staircase as two silhouettes came down and approached him, one tall and wide, the other short and hefty. The closer they drew the more they began to fill out in the dim light. The first thing he saw was the taller ones black Dickies and red Nike Cortez. The second one he saw was wearing a dress and flats. The duo stayed within the shadows. Even with their faces partially hidden, Te'Qui could still tell who they were: Wicked and Helen.

Te'Qui looked in Helen's direction with pleading eyes, mouthing to her to help him. Her eyes held guilt, but she quickly looked away. When he saw this, he hung his head. He knew that he was on his own to deal with whatever punishment was sent his way now.

Wicked sat a worn brown leather bag down on a table against the wall that looked like it was made to carry a bowling ball. With latex gloved hands, he unzipped the bag and began pulling out shiny silver tools that were made specifically for torture. One by one, he laid the tools on the old rusty iron table top until he drew the last. *Snikt.* He turned around to Te'Qui, smiling devilishly. The illumination from the dim light bulb in the ceiling bounced off of the instrument of death and a glare swept up its length.

Te'Qui eyes bulged and his mouth hung open. His heart raged inside of his chest, showing its impression on his left peck as it beat out of control. His head snapped from left to right. Helen dropped the spent beer can at her feet, crushed it with her flat and kicked it aside. Wicked advanced in his direction with the tool in his hand and evil thoughts on his mind. With nothing to lose, Te'Qui decided to make a run for it. He made a mad dash for the steps, but something caught him while in motion. He went up into the air and came down hard on his face, busting and bloodying his mouth. Licking his lips and swallowing, he tasted metal. He peeled open his eyelids just in time to see his red tooth tumbling up from him. He felt around inside his mouth and came across the space between his teeth. When he looked to his fingers they were stained with blood.

He looked to his ankle and saw that it had been shackled to the wall. When he looked up, Wicked and Helen were approaching him, laughing like a couple of crazed maniacs.

Te'Qui squeezed his eyelids closed and mouthed a prayer to himself, hoping that God Almighty would pull his black ass out of this one.

"The Lord can't save you lil' homie. Only you can," Wicked spoke honestly. "You either tell me who this cat is that gave you and bro bro that work, or I'm gonna make sure you get acquainted with each and every tool in that there bag behind me, ya dig?"

Te'Qui closed his eyes as he swallowed hard. He peeled them back open and stared up at his enemy with defiant eyes. If Wicked thought he was going to break under pressure, he was sadly mistaken. He knew that a man was only as good as his word and what he chose to live and die by. No matter what the sicko did to him he wouldn't fold, under any circumstances.

"Yeah, I dig and I still ain't telling you shit! Suck my dick!" He threw up both middle fingers, letting them linger. Although he was popping that shit, inside he was scared, but he couldn't show his abductor fear. Fuck no. Flashes of all of the good times he had with his family and Baby Wicked went through his mind. He wished he had one last chance to tell his parents how much he loved them. If only he could feel their embrace and hear them say it back. He would kill for that one moment. It was just too bad that the mad man before him was going to make sure that he never got it.

"Oh, I'm gonna love this," Wicked stated with a fiendish smile. He kicked the youngster in the chin, knocking him unconscious. He then pressed his sneaker against the little dude's chest and moved to perform surgery with the shiny instrument.

\*\*\*

Juvie was exactly where Gatz said he was, parlaying at the strip club acting a goddamn fool. He was shit face drunk, drinking champagne from the cracks of strippers' asses, and throwing singles like they were falling from out of the sky. When they rolled up on him, he was fiddling with his keys trying to unlock the door of his car. When he'd finally managed to pull it open, Uduka pounced out on him and clocked him across the back of the head with the butt of his gun. Before he could slink to the ground, the youngster caught him. With his brother's assistance, he dumped him in the trunk of his own car and drove off like they hadn't just kidnapped his mothafucking ass. Now here they were, an hour later with Don Juan's most trusted soldier in their possession.

"Uhhhh. Uhhhh." Juvie moaned as he slowly began to come to. He struggled to hold his head up, but once he got it upright his eyelids flickered and he looked over his surroundings, his head bobbing about. His vision was blurred so he only saw two distorted images before him. He squeezed his eyelids closed and popped them back open several times before he managed to identify who was in the room with him. He nearly leaped out of his skin when he saw Uche and Uduka standing before him, wearing less than friendly expressions. He didn't know who the fuck they were or why they had him hung up. Seeing the spear in the tallest ones hand he knew that either torture or death was in store for him. He only hoped it was the latter. Death. He prayed that it would be a quick one.

*Snikt! Snikt! Snikt!*

The sharp end of the spear sounded as the oldest of the Eme brothers sharpened it on a sharpening block. His eyes, as well as his baby brother's, were locked on Juvie. He could tell by the looks on their faces that they meant business. Oh yeah, there wasn't any mistaking that. He was sure he was in for a world of pain and his death would be right behind it. He swallowed hard, his heart beating so fast that he thought it was going to rupture. He went to move and found his wrists and ankles bound by ropes which were tied around the posts inside of the under construction tenement. His hands were wrapped up in so much duct tape that he couldn't ball his fingers into fists. They just stuck out, like the thorns of a rose. He knew his kidnappers had something sinister planned for him and he didn't want to be around to find out what it was.

Squinting his eyes and gritting his teeth, he pulled and tugged on his restraints, but there wasn't any use. He wasn't going anywhere. The ropes were secure and left him suspended in place. Feeling a cool breeze disturb the hairs of his nether region, he looked down and his eyes almost jumped out of his head. His dick and balls were exposed, hanging out of his zipper. He looked from his manhood then back up at the oldest of the Eme brothers. He was setting the sharpening block down and heading in his direction, his jaws were clenched so tight that he could see the bones in them.

Uche's hand shot out and gripped his capture's throat so tight that redness formed around his fingers. Veins rolled up Juvie's temples and his eyes bled tears. His head snapped from left to right as he was struggling to breathe. Believing this was his end, his arms and legs jerked violently as he attempted to escape. The tightness around his neck was like a noose, shutting off the oxygen to his brain.

With a pair of merciless eyes, Uche stared deep into the windows of his soul with a tight jaw. He watched him squirm against his death grip. *Psssssss!* He looked down and a yellow fluid was pelting his leg and his black leather shoes. That nigga was pissing on him! This angered him more and he squeezed his neck tighter, attempting to rip out his throat.

"Ya fuckin' insect…"

"Uche!" Uduka called out to him.

"…I'm going ta rip ya gotdamn throat out!"

"Uche! You keel 'em and we'll neva find Boxy's murderer," his younger brother reasoned.

Uche took a deep breath and relaxed a bit, releasing Juvie of his iron-like hand. *Shhhripppp!* He ripped the duct tape from off of his mouth, taking off the hairs of his light mustache and leaving a red streak behind. He grimaced, but ask the oldest African present did he give a fuck. *Hell No!*

"Alright muddafucka," he began, taking hold of his spear with both hands. "What we want ta know is where we can find dis Don Juan?"

Juvie stared up at him with defiance in his eyes.

"I've never heard of 'em."

*Snikt!*

*Thump!*

"Arghhh!" He gritted his teeth after having his index finger sliced off by the spear. Its movement was so fast it looked as if Uche hadn't raised his hand to use it.

"Where. Is. He?" he said like, *I'm not finna keep asking yo' mothafucking ass.*

"Why don't chu go ask yaaaaah!" He screamed at the top of his lungs with his head tilted back, you could see the pinkness of his mouth and all of his cavities, his beige teeth from years of smoking.

*Thump!* Another one of his fingers hit the floor.

"I can do dis all day, cock sucka! Try me!" he yelled, spit leaping from his lips.

Juvie looked up wincing and breathing hard, chest jumping wildly. His face coated with perspiration.

"Wat chu godda say now, tough guy, huh?"

"Your breath smells like goat sex! Hahahahaha." He busted up laughing, infecting Uche, who looked over his shoulder at his brother. He was laughing, too. And just that quick that pleasant expression was replaced. His forehead deepened with lines and his nose crinkled as his lips peeled back into a sneer, baring his teeth like a ferocious lion.

The spear whistled through the air hacking off fingers unevenly. *Snikt! Thump! Snikt! Thump! Snikt! Thump!* The severed fingers hit the surface one after another, making their own melody as they danced. By the time Uche was done playing butcher, all Juvie had was his thumbs left. He took a step back, holding his spear behind his back at an angle like he was about to attack again, his eyes never wavered from his victim. Through them it was as if he was saying *What now, smart ass?*

"You ready ta tell me sometin' now?" he asked, squared jaws pulsating, knuckles grasping the spear tighter, ready to decapitate his catch if he didn't talk.

Breathing hard, Juvie closed his eyes and made his lips into a tight line. Both of his hands were on fire with his fingers having been severed. The Nigerian butcher seemed to be having a grand old time chopping on him. Once he was through with his hands, he'd most likely get to hacking off his toes and so on and so forth. He couldn't have that, living life never being able to hold anything or walk again. Nah, to hell with that, he'd much rather drop a dime.

Juvie nodded his head to Uche's question and said, "Okay, okay…"

***

Ta'shauna stood out on the terrace of Faison's Malibu home, dressed in a white floral knitted gown. Her pretty pedicured feet gripped the cool granite tiled floor, while her hands held on to the ledge as she faced the ocean. Although she couldn't see the view before her, she could imagine it. Her mind spun images of what the scenery could be, hearing the water crash into the shores of the sandy beach and smelling the faint traces of salt in the air. A smile emerged on her face as she inhaled the fresh air and then exhaled.

Suddenly, she became deathly still and her smile disappeared. Her eyes darted to their corners and fear gripped her heart. She couldn't see him, but he'd just entered the bedroom. She could smell him. The scent of his aftershave gave him away as soon as he darkened the doorway. She'd never forget that after shave, he'd worn it the three years they'd been together.

"Tiaz?" She gasped and turned around.

Tranay Adams

# Chapter Seventeen
## *Hour later*

Lil' Stan lay back in bed with his hands clasped behind his head, looking down between his legs. His dick was standing straight up through the hole in his boxer briefs. Its bulbous head throbbing as it slightly twitched, it was so stiff. His member was harder than it had ever been in his entire life and with good purpose too. Tonight he was going to get a shot of pussy and some scalp he'd been chasing since high school. Sure it may have cost him a stack, but to him it was well worth it. At least he hoped. When he fell through King Henry's that night, he had only planned on throwing back a few drinks and tricking a few dollars on a couple lap dances and a blow job. See, Southern California's strip club scenery had grown quite boring to him. He'd hit every gentlemen's club out there and more than one of the girls worked at the same ones. King Henry's was sort of new to him though. He only breezed through on rare occasions when he wanted a taste of some variety. Now don't get it fucked up, he loved his black women to death, but sometimes a nigga wanted to sample a little something different, every now and again.

Lil' Stan wasn't expecting much to write home about. So imagine the look on his face when he sat at the front of the stage with a black bottle of Belaire and three hundred dollars in singles, and saw his high school crush take the stage, butt naked. He was mesmerized. Poochie had always been a slim girl, but now her pretty caramel ass was as thick as a brick shit house. She had ass for days and titties for weeks. She wore hazel contacts and rocked a golden brown, lengthy wavy wig that reached her ample bottom. The bitch looked like one of those World Star models. Stretch marks, stab wounds, cigarette burns and all. But goddamn she was finer than frog's hair.

The bathroom door opened and the light shined on the back of the vixen. Although she was a silhouette in the dimly lit bedroom, the illumination at her back filled out all of the curves and grooves of her thick body. Flipping the light switch off, she crossed the threshold as nude as she was on the stage that night, contacts and wig included. She climbed upon the bed and crawled toward him slowly, with her head tilted downward, licking her full lips and looking like a hungry panther. A smile broadened Lil' Stan's lips and his dick grew even harder. He twiddled his toes in anticipation of feeling her mouth engulf him. He was so excited that his head oozed with pre-cum. When she reached him, she grabbed a hold of his member and rubbed the semen around its head. She then opened her mouth, her saliva looking like webs as she parted her lips. He bit down on his inner jaw, feeling the heat from her grill as she brought her mouth to him. He jumped a little when her warm salivating mouth swallowed him, taking him into the back of her throat where he felt the vibration of her humming. He could literally feel her tonsils. He closed his eyes and tilted his head back, savoring the moment.

"Sssssss, shit, that's what I'm talking about." His nostrils flared and he breathed heavily. She stared up at his face, making a whole lot of slurping and sucking sounds as her manicured hands, swept up and down his stomach. Her mouth went up and down his meat rapidly. She squeezed his dick, twisting and turning it as she glided her lips up and down it. This made him sit up and look down at her with a shocked expression plastered across his face. His eyes were bugged and his mouth was quivering. He reached for her head, but she grabbed his hand and held it down, continuing to work her jaws.

"Mmmm." She made the sensual noise, squishing and sloshing sounds filling the bedroom. When he reached with his other hand, she held that one down too, going on about her business.

His head dropped back into the pillow and his eyes rolled as his mouth hung open.

"Oh my fucking God, what're you doing to me?" he uttered, sounding like he was exhausted, listening to all of the nasty noises she was making as she enveloped his meat.

"I'm 'bout to make you cum, baby," she said with a mouthful of spit before letting the hot saliva roll off of her tongue and coat the head of his member. Using the goo, she stroked him up and down, wrinkling and straightening his dick. Her hair kept falling into her face, so she stopped which garnered the side eye from him, but she assured him that she was going to finish her business.

"Hold on a second, boo." She held up a finger as she reached for the dresser, grabbing a rubber band. She pulled her hair back into a ponytail and tangled the band around it, then went back to the task at hand, making the young nigga bust off. He clawed at the sheets and pushed off of the bed, banging his head against the headboard trying to get away from her. She had to hold his waist down until she finished the job. She whipped her head on him, causing him to squirm and moan.

"Yeah, nigga, gimme what cha got, gimme what I want," she said between sucking and jerking his meat.

"Ahhhh, shit, I'm finna cum, I'm finna bust this nut!" His eyes were white and he was rising at the waist, further and further. Veins bulged in his neck and his toes curled tightly, making fists. When he came, his big toes pointed and he fell back in bed, turning his head. He panted hard as she continued to slurp up the last of his babies. There was a loud suction sound when she withdrew her lips and straddled him. She smacked him across his face a couple of times and he looked to her with hooded eyes like *huh?* It looked like he had fallen asleep. She showed him the off white semen she had cupped on her tongue and then swallowed it. She wiped her mouth with the back of her hand and followed his instructions to ride his face.

He jerked his hardness, getting it back harder as his mouth awaited her bald, pierced pussy. She was about to lower her pulsating cunt onto his lips when his cell phone rang and vibrated, putting her on pause.

"You wanna get that, sweetie, or should we continue?" She looked from him to the cell phone on the nightstand.

Lil' Stan looked from the cell phone to her then back again. He didn't want to answer it, but from the tune it was playing he knew it was Don Juan.

"Damn." He fumed, crawling over to his cell phone and picking it up. It was indeed Don. He answered.

"What's up with it?"

"Have you seen Juvie?" Don Juan asked.

"Nah," Lil' Stan frowned. "I thought he had that thing witchu."

"He did, but that nigga hasn't been answering," he responded. "I done called 'em like fifty million times and shit. But yo' fuck it. Get dressed, we're 'bout to bust this move."

Lil' Stan looked at the bodacious, caramel skinned beauty lying beside him playing in her pussy. Her head was tilted all of the way back so that he could see underneath her chin and she was whining and purring. Her pussy was running like a broken faucet and her French tipped pedicured toenails were curled. She was taking herself to ecstasy. Lil' Stan licked his lips thirstily and continued groping his hard-on. He couldn't wait to feel the comfort of her warm, wet walls, hugging him like a relative at a family reunion.

"Aye, Don, gimme like fifteen minutes, homie, and we can roll out." He spoke with his eyes still lingering on his conquest for the night.

"Nigga, bring yo' ass outta the house now, I'm parked out front!"

Lil' Stan looked at his cell phone with a twisted face like *Nigga please.* "Yeah, alright." He pressed *end*, disconnecting the call. He then tossed the cell on the dresser.

*Honk! Honk! Honk! Honk!* Don Juan blew the horn violently from outside.

The young nigga didn't pay the honking any mind as he slithered over to old girl, removing her fingers from her cunt and spreading her legs apart. He opened his mouth and latched onto her treasure, sucking on it like it was Ramen noodles and making humming noises. "Ahhhh, ssssss." She enjoyed his devouring of her pearl, massaging the back of his head. She held up her ripe, melon breast with one hand and sucked on her nipple, her eyes rolling to the back of her head, making her look like a demon spirit had taken possession of her. While all of this was going on, there was a lot of racket inside of the house, but they were too engrossed within the palace of pleasure to pay attention.

Heavy footfalls made their way down the hallway until they sounded like they were right at the door. *Boom!* The bedroom door swung open, bouncing off of the wall and startling Lil' Stan and his sex partner.

"Get cho shit and get dressed," Don Juan ordered. "There's killing that needs to be done."

He sat down on the bed and watched his little homie scramble to his feet and slip on his gray Dickies, one leg at a time as he talked shit under his breath.

"You got something on yo' mind, pimpin'?"

"Nah," he replied with arched eyebrows and twisted lips, zipping up his pants.

"Good." Don Juan lay back in bed and looked up at the ebony vixen. He smiled and puckered his lips at her, before lifting up the bed sheets and ogling her goods. He whistled and turned to Lil' Stan. "I see why you didn't wanna come out, my nigga." She snatched the sheet down.

Don Juan held no regard for how homegirl felt. She was nothing more than a piece of ass to him, a human cum dumpster. He'd tricked off with her more times than he cared to remember.

A perturbed Lil' Stan, tucked his gun on his waistline and threw his hood on his head. Pulling a knot of dead presidents from out of his pocket, he peeled off a few and tossed them on the bed beside his latest conquest.

"Take a cab home, I'll get up witchu later." He told her. Watching her snatch up the money and count it. She hurriedly slipped on her clothes and grabbed her hooker boots, hurrying out of the door on her bare pedicured feet.

Lil' Stan slid a pair of black sunglasses on his face and looked to Don Juan.

"Let's roll, nigga."

"Roll, we shall." Don Juan followed him out of the door.

He and Lil' Stan were on their way to pay Tiaz a visit.

***

Kiana twisted the dial and turned off the showerhead. She stepped out of the tub one foot at a time, singing and grabbing the towel off of the rack. She dried off thoroughly and rubbed out a clear space in the medicine cabinet mirror so that she could see her reflection. She plucked her toothbrush from out of the cabinet and picked up the toothpaste. Once she was done taking care of her hygiene, she danced out of the bathroom in her bath towel across the threshold crooning the lyrics to Tony Braxton's *I Get So High.*

*Oh I get so high*
*When I'm around you baby I can touch the sky*
*You make my temperature rise*
*You're makin' me high Oh (baby baby baby baby)*
*I want to feel your heart and soul inside of me*
*Let's make a deal you roll, I lick*
*And we can go flying into ecstasy*
*Oh darlin' you and me*
*Light my fire*
*Blow my flame*
*Take me, take me, take me away...*

Kiana journeyed down the hallway and bent the corner into the baby's bedroom. Reciting the lyrics, she flipped on the lightswitch and her heart dropped.

"Ahhhhhh!" she screamed, causing her uvula to shake and her eyes to bulge in terror. Tiaz was standing by the baby's crib, rocking him in one arm while gripping his banger with the other. His head snapped up hearing the shrill and he narrowed his eyelids, shooting her a menacing glare that warned her to shut the fuck up or there would be consequences and repercussions.

"Shhhh." He held the gun to his lips, telling her to be quiet. "Keep it down or you'll wake lil' man."

Kiana snatched the lamp off of the dresser and charged toward him screaming, "Mothafuckaaaaa!"

He jabbed her in the eye with the barrel of his weapon, dropping her to the floor. She lay there moaning in pain. Swiftly, he kicked her in the ribs and stomped her on the temple, knocking her out cold. He then left the baby's bedroom and returned with her cell phone. Sitting down in a chair, he scrolled until he found the number he was looking for and sent a text message.

***

After making sure the address matched the one that they had, Lil' Stan pulled into the alley behind Tiaz's house and killed the engine. He and Don Juan pulled bandanas with the skull mouths over the lower halves of their faces. He then dipped his hand beneath the seat, coming back up one at a time with a machete. *Snikt! Snikt!* He held tight to one and passed the other to Lil' Stan.

"Fuck is this?" Lil' Stan frowned.

"A machete."

"I know that, but I thought we were gone use the burners."

"Nah, this mothafucka deserves the blades for fucking with my business." He opened the door and said, "Bring yo' ass, nigga."

They jumped out of the car and hopped the gate into Tiaz's backyard. Hunched over, they moved as stealthily as thieves cloaked in the darkness, machetes at the ready. They crept up the steps of the back porch and placed their ears to the door. Hearing voices inside, Don Juan took a step back and looked to his accomplice. He held up four fingers and counted down. Once he dropped the last finger, he kicked the door in as hard as he could. The door swung open and slammed into the wall. They ran inside, machetes gripped, eager to chop a nigga up like a brick of dope.

Hearing the voices coming from the living room, they thought that they had him cornered, but once they crossed the threshold coming from out of the kitchen, they saw they were mistaken. The lights were off and the flat screen was playing *The Game of Thrones*. With a hand gesture like an umpire, Don Juan gave Lil' Stan instructions to check the bedroom upstairs while he searched the ones downstairs. Once they were done with their search they met back up in the living room. They looked to one another shaking their heads. Tiaz wasn't anywhere in sight.

Frustrated, Don Juan plopped down on the couch and pulled the bandana down from the lower half of his face. His eyebrows arched and he bit down on the corner of his lip, gripping the handle of his machete so tight that his knuckles crackled. He wanted Tiaz's ass badder than he'd wanted his first nut.

"Grrrr." A low growl manifested under his breath and suddenly he swung his machete at a neighboring lamp. It shattered, spilling broken pieces and sending the shade flying across the living room. "Where the fuck is this nigga, man?"

Don Juan's cell phone chimed with a text message. Nostrils flaring and chest heaving, he grabbed his cell phone and looked at the screen.

*hurry home. sumthin is wrng wit the bby.*

"Come on!" He shot out of the living room, heading for the backdoor with Lil' Stan on his heels.

***

*Scurrrrr!*

Don Juan brought the Porsche truck to a halt, parking across the street from the condo, since no closer parking spaces were available. He and Lil' Stan hopped out. They jogged across the street, narrowly missing being hit by cars. Hearing screams coming from above, they looked up and were devastated at what they saw. Tiaz was standing in the window, wearing a black bandana over the lower half of his face. In one hand he held a gun and in the other he held tightly to the back of a naked Kiana's neck as she struggled to get away. He cracked her upside the head with his banger to get her to stop resisting. She grimaced and cried, tears rolling over her lips and dripping.

"Wait! Hold up!" Don Juan panicked, scared for his wife's life.

"To hell with holding up! You fuck with the bull, you get the horns, homes!" Tiaz spat unmercifully. He tucked his head bussa and looped a noose around Kiana's neck. He then kicked her out of the window. The wind blew upwards, ruffling her hair as she screamed to high heaven, eyes stretched wide open. She flailed her arms and her legs, moving as if she was running on air.

"Noooooooooo!" Don Juan bellowed, with horror etched across his face.

*To Be Continued...*
Bury Me A G III
Crucified by The Streets

# Submission Guideline

Submit the first three chapters of your completed manuscript to ldpsubmissions@gmail.com, subject line: Your book's title. The manuscript must be in a .doc file and sent as an attachment. Document should be in Times New Roman, double spaced and in size 12 font. Also, provide your synopsis and full contact information. If sending multiple submissions, they must each be in a separate email.

Have a story but no way to send it electronically? You can still submit to LDP/Ca$h Presents. Send in the first three chapters, written or typed, of your completed manuscript to:

**LDP: Submissions Dept**

Tranay Adams

**Po Box 870494**
**Mesquite, Tx 75187**

*DO NOT send original manuscript. Must be a duplicate.*

Provide your synopsis and a cover letter containing your full contact information.

Thanks for considering LDP and Ca$h Presents.

Bury Me A G 2

Tranay Adams

**Coming Soon from Lock Down Publications/Ca$h Presents**

BOW DOWN TO MY GANGSTA
By **Ca$h**
TORN BETWEEN TWO
By **Coffee**
BLOOD STAINS OF A SHOTTA **III**
By **Jamaica**
STEADY MOBBIN **III**
By **Marcellus Allen**
BLOOD OF A BOSS **V**
By **Askari**
LOYAL TO THE GAME **IV**
LIFE OF SIN II
By **T.J. & Jelissa**
A DOPEBOY'S PRAYER **II**
By **Eddie "Wolf" Lee**
IF LOVING YOU IS WRONG... **III**
LOVE ME EVEN WHEN IT HURTS **II**
By **Jelissa**
TRUE SAVAGE **VII**
By **Chris Green**
BLAST FOR ME **III**
A BRONX TALE III
DUFFLE BAG CARTEL
By **Ghost**
ADDICTIED TO THE DRAMA **III**

220

By **Jamila Mathis**

LIPSTICK KILLAH **III**

WHAT BAD BITCHES DO **III**

KILL ZONE **II**

By **Aryanna**

THE COST OF LOYALTY **II**

By **Kweli**

SHE FELL IN LOVE WITH A REAL ONE **II**

By **Tamara Butler**

RENEGADE BOYS **III**

By **Meesha**

CORRUPTED BY A GANGSTA **IV**

By **Destiny Skai**

A GANGSTER'S CODE **III**

By **J-Blunt**

KING OF NEW YORK IV

RISE TO POWER II

By **T.J. Edwards**

GORILLAS IN THE BAY II

**De'Kari**

THE STREETS ARE CALLING II

**Duquie Wilson**

KINGPIN KILLAZ III

**Hood Rich**

STEADY MOBBIN' **III**

**Marcellus Allen**

SINS OF A HUSTLA II

**ASAD**

CASH MONEY HOES

**Nicole Goosby**

TRIGGADALE II

**Elijah R. Freeman**

MARRIED TO A BOSS 2…

**By Destiny Skai & Chris Green**

KINGS OF THE GAME II

**Playa Ray**

<u>**Available Now**</u>

<u>RESTRAINING ORDER **I & II**</u>

By **CA$H & Coffee**

<u>LOVE KNOWS NO BOUNDARIES **I II & III**</u>

By **Coffee**

<u>RAISED AS A GOON I, II,  III & IV</u>

<u>BRED BY THE SLUMS I, II, III</u>

<u>BLAST FOR ME I & II</u>

<u>ROTTEN TO THE CORE I III</u>

<u>A BRONX TALE I, II</u>

By **Ghost**

<u>LAY IT DOWN **I & II**</u>

<u>LAST OF A DYING BREED</u>

<u>BLOOD STAINS OF A SHOTTA I & II</u>

By **Jamaica**

<u>LOYAL TO THE GAME</u>

LOYAL TO THE GAME II

LOYAL TO THE GAME III

LIFE OF SIN

By **TJ & Jelissa**

BLOODY COMMAS I & II

SKI MASK CARTEL I  II & III

KING OF NEW YORK I II,III

RISE TO POWER


By **T.J. Edwards**

IF LOVING HIM IS WRONG…I & II

LOVE ME EVEN WHEN IT HURTS

By **Jelissa**

WHEN THE STREETS CLAP BACK I & II III

By **Jibril Williams**

A DISTINGUISHED THUG STOLE MY HEART I II & III

LOVE SHOULDN'T HURT I II III

RENEGADE BOYS I & II

By **Meesha**

A GANGSTER'S CODE I & II

**By J-Blunt**

PUSH IT TO THE LIMIT

By **Bre' Hayes**

BLOOD OF A BOSS **I, II, III & IV**

By **Askari**

THE STREETS BLEED MURDER **I, II & III**

THE HEART OF A GANGSTA I II& III

223

By **Jerry Jackson**

CUM FOR ME

CUM FOR ME 2

CUM FOR ME 3

CUM FOR ME 4

An **LDP Erotica Collaboration**

BRIDE OF A HUSTLA **I  II & II**

THE FETTI GIRLS **I, II& III**

CORRUPTED BY A GANGSTA I, II & III

By **Destiny Skai**

WHEN A GOOD GIRL GOES BAD

By **Adrienne**

A GANGSTER'S REVENGE **I II III & IV**

THE BOSS MAN'S DAUGHTERS

THE BOSS MAN'S DAUGHTERS II

THE BOSSMAN'S DAUGHTERS III

THE BOSSMAN'S DAUGHTERS IV

THE BOSS MAN'S DAUGHTERS **V**

A SAVAGE LOVE  **I & II**

BAE BELONGS TO ME

A HUSTLER'S DECEIT I, II

WHAT BAD BITCHES DO I, II

By **Aryanna**

A KINGPIN'S AMBITON

A KINGPIN'S AMBITION **II**

I MURDER FOR THE DOUGH

By **Ambitious**

TRUE SAVAGE

TRUE SAVAGE II

TRUE SAVAGE **III**

TRUE SAVAGE **IV**

TRUE SAVAGE **V**

TRUE SAVAGE **VI**

By **Chris Green**

A DOPEBOY'S PRAYER

By **Eddie "Wolf" Lee**

THE KING CARTEL **I, II & III**

By **Frank Gresham**

THESE NIGGAS AIN'T LOYAL **I, II & III**

By **Nikki Tee**

GANGSTA SHYT **I II &III**

By **CATO**

THE ULTIMATE BETRAYAL

By **Phoenix**

BOSS'N UP **I , II & III**

By **Royal Nicole**

I LOVE YOU TO DEATH

**By Destiny J**

I RIDE FOR MY HITTA

I STILL RIDE FOR MY HITTA

By **Misty Holt**

LOVE & CHASIN' PAPER

By **Qay Crockett**

TO DIE IN VAIN

**SINS OF A HUSTLA**

By **ASAD**

BROOKLYN HUSTLAZ

By **Boogsy Morina**

BROOKLYN ON LOCK I & II

By **Sonovia**

GANGSTA CITY

By **Teddy Duke**

A DRUG KING AND HIS DIAMOND I & II III

A DOPEMAN'S RICHES

HER MAN, MINE'S TOO I, II

**By Nicole Goosby**

TRAPHOUSE KING **I II & III**

KINGPIN KILLAZ

By **Hood Rich**

LIPSTICK KILLAH **I, II**

CRIME OF PASSION I & II

By **Mimi**

STEADY MOBBN' **I, II**

By **Marcellus Allen**

WHO SHOT YA **I, II**

**Renta**

GORILLAZ IN THE BAY

**DE'KARI**

TRIGGADALE

**Elijah R. Freeman**

GOD BLESS THE TRAPPERS I, II, III

THESE SCANDALOUS STREETS I, II, III

FEAR MY GANGSTA I, II, III

THESE STREETS DON'T LOVE NOBODY I, II

**Tranay Adams**

THE STREETS ARE CALLING

**Duquie Wilson**

MARRIED TO A BOSS…

**By Destiny Skai & Chris Green**

KINGS OF THE GAME II

**Playa Ray**

Tranay Adams

## BOOKS BY LDP'S CEO, CA$H

TRUST IN NO MAN

TRUST IN NO MAN 2

TRUST IN NO MAN 3

BONDED BY BLOOD

SHORTY GOT A THUG

THUGS CRY

THUGS CRY 2

THUGS CRY 3

TRUST NO BITCH

TRUST NO BITCH 2

TRUST NO BITCH 3

TIL MY CASKET DROPS

RESTRAINING ORDER

RESTRAINING ORDER 2

IN LOVE WITH A CONVICT

**Coming Soon**

BONDED BY BLOOD 2

BOW DOWN TO MY GANGSTA

Tranay Adams

Made in the USA
Columbia, SC
14 July 2023

20425515R00127